PUFFIN BOOKS

After

Morris Gleitzman grew up in England and went to live in Australia when he was sixteen. He worked as a frozen-chicken thawer, sugar-mill rolling-stock unhooker, fashion-industry trainee, department-store Santa, TV producer, newspaper columnist and screenwriter. Then he had a wonderful experience. He wrote a novel for young people. Now he's one of the bestselling children's authors in Australia. He lives in Melbourne, but visits Britain regularly. His many books include *Two Weeks with the Queen*, *Water Wings*, *Bumface*, *Boy Overboard* and *Once*.

Visit Morris at his website:
morrisgleitzman.com

Also by Morris Gleitzman

After

MORRIS GLEITZMAN

PUFFIN

PUFFIN BOOKS

Published by the Penguin Group
Penguin Books Ltd, 80 Strand, London WC2R 0RL, England
Penguin Group (USA) Inc., 375 Hudson Street, New York, New York 10014, USA
Penguin Group (Canada), 90 Eglinton Avenue East, Suite 700, Toronto, Ontario, Canada M4P 2Y3
(a division of Pearson Penguin Canada Inc.)
Penguin Ireland, 25 St Stephen's Green, Dublin 2, Ireland (a division of Penguin Books Ltd)
Penguin Group (Australia), 250 Camberwell Road, Camberwell, Victoria 3124, Australia
(a division of Pearson Australia Group Pty Ltd)
Penguin Books India Pvt Ltd, 11 Community Centre, Panchsheel Park, New Delhi – 110 017, India
Penguin Group (NZ), 67 Apollo Drive, Rosedale, Auckland 0632, New Zealand
(a division of Pearson New Zealand Ltd)
Penguin Books (South Africa) (Pty) Ltd, Block D, Rosebank Office Park, 181 Jan Smuts Avenue,
Parktown North, Gauteng 2193, South Africa

Penguin Books Ltd, Registered Offices: 80 Strand, London WC2R 0RL, England

puffinbooks.com

Published in Australia by Penguin Group (Australia) 2012
Published in Great Britain in Puffin Books 2012
004

Text copyright © Gleitzman McCaul Pty Ltd, 2012
All rights reserved

The moral right of the author has been asserted

Set in 13/15.5 Minion by Post Pre-Press Group, Brisbane, Queensland
Printed in Great Britain by Clays Ltd, St Ives plc

British Library Cataloguing in Publication Data
A CIP catalogue record for this book is available from the British Library

ISBN: 978-0-141-34313-6

www.greenpenguin.co.uk

ALWAYS LEARNING   **PEARSON**

For all the parents

After I woke up and had a stretch as usual and got dirt under my fingernails as usual, I heard voices above me in the barn.

Lots of voices.

Which wasn't usual at all.

I held my breath in the dark and tried not to make any scared noises.

You know how when there's a war and you hide in a hole for two years so the Nazis won't find you and each night a kind man called Gabriek brings you food and water and takes your wees and poos away and the only voice you ever hear is his and you don't want to hear anybody else's because that could mean the Nazis know where you are and they've come to get you?

I think the Nazis have come to get me.

The voices up there sound bossy and impatient and angry.

I sit up on my mattress and listen hard to catch

1

what they're saying. I try to make out if they're using Nazi expressions like *Jew vermin* and *shoot him in the vermin head*. But I can't hear properly because this hole is under a horse stall and Dom is a big horse and he's muffling the sound.

I struggle to stay calm and think who else the people could be. Neighbours from the next farm wanting to borrow some turnips? The choir from the local church trying to persuade Gabriek to join?

I look at the luminous watch Gabriek gave me.

Five past six.

It's evening. In the middle of winter. Normal people don't go out at all in winter if they can help it, and definitely not after dark.

The men up there must be Nazis.

I try to make myself as small as I can in my hole, which isn't easy because I've been growing a bit lately. Plus at the moment my body is completely rigid with fear.

This is what I've been dreading. This is what I've been trying not to think about.

Why did the Nazis have to come today?

On my birthday.

Maybe they're doing it on purpose. Maybe they've got a Jewish birthday list. Maybe for Nazis it's extra fun to kill people on their special day.

I get cramp in my leg.

Ow.

I rub it as quietly as I can. I wish the straw in this mattress wasn't so scratchy and noisy. You'd think

2

in 1945 they'd have invented quieter straw. And I wish I wasn't surrounded by things that go clink and clunk. Pee bottles and Richmal Crompton books and the small pieces of machinery Gabriek gives me to explore with my hands when the candle runs out so I can get an education.

All that education will be wasted if I die now.

I try to breathe very softly. I try to relax and take my mind off things by thinking about the hydraulic valve system in a hand-operated water pump.

It doesn't work.

I'm still feeling scared.

Not just of being shot. I'm even more scared of what will happen to Gabriek if the Nazis find me here. The Nazis hate people who protect Jews. They shoot them too, but they do worse things to them first.

The voices up there sound like they're arguing.

I still can't make out what they're saying. I hope Gabriek's telling the Nazis the story we made up, the one about how they should stay away from Dom's stall because Dom is a moody horse with a very catching skin condition.

Which isn't true, but you have to lie to Nazis, it's the only way.

I try something else to stop myself panicking. It's what I do when I have a lot of loneliness or fear or worry. I close my eyes and pretend I'm William from the Richmal Crompton books. Having adventures in the woods with my friends. Cooking

3

on campfires and building tree houses and inventing irrigation systems to help ants grow crops.

Now I'm thirteen I'm probably a bit old for that, but I don't care.

Except it's not working either.

I hear a sound up above. A loud metallic sound. I know what that sound is. The safety catch on a gun.

I feel sick.

I think about a story Mum read me when I was little. About a fieldmouse who was going to be killed by a dragon. Instead of cowering in the dry leaves, the mouse decided to look death in the face.

I bet Mum and Dad did that when the Nazis murdered them in the death camp.

It's what I've decided to do if the Nazis murder me. Keep my eyes wide open and look death in the face like Mum and Dad did.

Plus that way, if there's a chance to escape, I'll see it.

The voices up there are getting louder. One of them is definitely Gabriek. And I can hear the other voices more clearly now as well.

Wait a minute.

Everyone's speaking Polish. Nazis usually speak German. It's very unusual for them to speak Polish.

What's going on?

I feel around for my glasses, put them on and gently tug on the security pulley system Gabriek made. Above my head the trapdoor opens just a bit.

I wait for lumps of horse poo to fall in like they always do, then I carefully kneel up and peek out.

And almost faint.

In front of my face, sitting on the sawdust between Dom's back hooves, is a small parcel wrapped in one of Gabriek's hankies and tied with string.

A birthday present.

Gabriek must have left it there to surprise me when I come out for my meal later.

If any Nazis see it, I'm finished.

I open the trapdoor a fraction more, grab the present and stuff it into my pocket.

Then I peer out to make sure nobody saw it.

My glasses are smudged and cracked, and Dom's back legs are blocking part of my vision, but I can still see what's going on.

Except I don't understand what I'm seeing.

There are about six men surrounding Gabriek. They've all got guns and torches, but they're not wearing Nazi uniforms, just ordinary clothes. And they look too tough and fierce to be hungry neighbours or grumpy choir members.

Who are they?

Why are they so angry with Gabriek?

Another person steps into view. She must have been there all the time, but I couldn't see her behind Dom's big shoulders.

I stare.

Mum?

I go weak with shock and the rope slips out of my hand and I grab it again just in time to stop the trapdoor slamming shut.

I stare some more.

It's not Mum. It's just a woman who looks sort of like Mum did when Mum was younger. Mostly because she's wearing a red headscarf like one of Mum's. But this woman is about twenty and Mum would be much older than that if she wasn't dead. Plus this woman is wearing a leather jacket with a gun over her shoulder, and Mum didn't like leather jackets or guns.

One of the men grabs Gabriek by the arm and pushes him towards the door.

Gabriek doesn't fight back.

I realise what's happening.

Whoever these people are, they don't know I'm here. Gabriek's letting them take him to protect me.

They all leave the barn together, Gabriek and the men and the woman.

I close the trapdoor and huddle back onto my mattress. I'm shivering now and not just because it's always cold in this hole.

I've guessed who those people are.

The Polish secret police.

I learned about the Polish secret police from one of the old newspapers Gabriek put in here to try to soak up some of the damp.

The Polish secret police are on the Nazis' side. One of the jobs they do for the Nazis is arrest Polish slave workers who've escaped from Germany.

Gabriek was a slave worker, and he escaped from Germany.

In my imagination I ask Richmal Crompton for her help. So Gabriek can escape again.

'Felix.'

I jump, startled.

It's Gabriek's voice.

That was quick.

'Felix, listen,' says Gabriek quietly.

He must be crouching close to the trapdoor so nobody else can hear him.

'I can't bring your birthday meal just at the moment,' he says. 'I have to go out for a while with our visitors.'

I hear the clank of Dom's bucket.

My insides sag.

Gabriek hasn't escaped. He's probably just told the secret police he has to pop back into the barn for a moment to feed Dom. So he can secretly try to stop me worrying.

'Do you hear me?' says Gabriek. 'Felix?'

'Yes,' I say.

'Try to sleep some more,' says Gabriek. 'Or do some education.'

I hear Dom nuzzling into his bucket again, but I don't hear anything else from Gabriek.

He must have gone back out to the secret police.

Who'll hand him over to the Nazis.

My insides ache with worry.

I don't want Gabriek to sacrifice himself to protect me.

If the Nazis catch me they'll just shoot me. But when they catch escaped slave workers, they hurt them badly and stick up photos of their crippled bodies in Germany as a warning to all the other slave workers there.

It was in the paper.

I don't want them to do that to Gabriek.

So I don't have any choice.

I have to try to rescue him.

After a quick listen to make sure the secret police hadn't come back into the barn, I went to rescue Gabriek.

Or tried to.

The trapdoor wouldn't open.

I knew why. Dom must be standing on it. When a horse is standing on your trapdoor, forget trying to push it up, you won't be able to.

Urgently I jiggle the pulley rope in a special way that makes the security lock rattle. It's a signal between me and Dom.

I hear a clunk as Dom steps off the trapdoor.

I push it open and climb out.

Ow.

It always hurts, climbing out. When you live in a hole your legs get weak and painful because the muscles stop growing properly, even if you do thirty minutes of walking round the barn every night like I do.

'Thanks, Dom,' I say, and give him a pat.

I'm lucky to have a friend like him.

I can see from the glint in his eyes he wants to help me rescue Gabriek. For a moment I'm tempted. Dom's a workhorse and not that fast, but riding him would still be quicker than trying to chase secret police on legs like mine.

Except I think my only hope is to stay out of sight until I work out how to do the rescue. It'd be really hard to keep a big horse like Dom hidden, even at night.

'Sorry, Dom,' I say.

Dom snorts softly and I can see he understands. I can also see he's telling me something with his breath, which is white in the wintry air.

'Good thought,' I say to him. 'Thanks.'

I grab one of my blankets from the hole. Then I close the trapdoor, say goodbye to Dom and make sure the gate to his stall is latched tight.

As I hurry towards the barn door, I listen anxiously for the sound of an engine. If the secret police came by car, I won't have a hope. They'll drive Gabriek to a Nazi dungeon in town before I can even get to the farm gate.

But I can't hear any engines, not even in the distance.

Luckily the one thing that does improve when you live in a hole is your hearing. Well, two things, because you also get pretty good at seeing in the dark. Which is just as well for me because these glasses are cracked, and I've had them since I was ten, so sometimes things are a bit blurry.

I start to open the barn door, then stop.

I haven't been out of this barn for two years.

Suddenly I'm scared.

I remind myself that Gabriek needs me. I didn't have the chance to save Mum and Dad from the Nazis. Or Zelda, or Barney, or Genia. But I do have the chance with Gabriek.

I go outside.

And stop again.

Outside is huge.

The sky is everywhere, crammed with stars.

I haven't seen anything like this for so long, not even all those times in the hole when I closed my eyes and pushed my fists into my eye sockets for entertainment.

But I'm not here for entertainment now.

I peer down the track towards the farm gate. No car lights, no torches, nothing. I scan the fields all around, acres of frosty cabbage stumps twinkling in the moonlight.

There. On the other side of that field. Dark shapes moving across the stumps.

But that's the wrong direction.

Why are they taking Gabriek away from town?

Of course. They must be heading for the forest. The Nazis like to shoot people in forests. I think it's to save making the graveyards in town overcrowded. Probably the same thing happens when the Nazis want to hurt people badly. They probably do that in forests too, so people in town won't be woken up by the cries of pain.

The Nazis must be doing forest shooting and hurting tonight, which is why the secret police are working late.

I wrap the blanket round me and go after them.

My legs hurt.

I don't mind because I'm managing to keep up with the dark figures who are hurrying across the fields ahead of me.

I'm praying the secret police don't hear me and turn round.

Please, Richmal Crompton, make it so those secret police haven't done any special training to improve their hearing.

I wish I had better boots. These fields are frozen and rough. I'm not complaining though. People in holes should leave the best boots for people who need to run for their lives, that's only fair.

Nobody up ahead looks like they're running for their life. Or lagging behind, or being dragged. Gabriek must be co-operating. Probably to get the secret police as far away from the barn as possible.

I try to keep my breathing regular so I have enough oxygen in my legs to keep up.

It's hard to breathe properly when the air's this cold. And when you think about a person like Gabriek being maimed or crippled. A brave kind loving person who risks his safety every day to protect a kid who isn't even his real-life son.

I wish Gabriek had some weapons to help him escape. But he's not interested in weapons. He's only interested in mending things. He's a genius at that. Machinery, animal equipment, electrical objects, anything except weapons.

If my best friend Zelda had met him, she'd have called him a mending person. Zelda was only six but she had the loving heart of a ten-year-old and she knew when a person was good.

That's another reason Gabriek has to be kept safe. The world needs all the mending people it can get at the moment. There are too many people around who just break things.

Well, I'm an imagining person, and I'm going to use my imagination to work out a way to stop the Nazis hurting Gabriek.

I can do it, I know I can, as long as those secret police stay in the open where I can see them and don't go into the forest.

They've gone into the forest.

It's much harder to follow them in here.

Before it was just field after field after field. All flat. All moonlit.

Now it's trees after trees after trees. This forest path is dark and winding and hilly and I can't see far enough ahead to spot them. Plus forests aren't as cold as fields and there isn't any frost on the ground for footprints. Even my very good hearing isn't helping me.

No footsteps, no voices, nothing.

At least that means they probably haven't started hurting Gabriek yet.

I have to find them. I've thought of a way to save Gabriek and I need to do it before it's too late.

Before I get too scared and change my mind.

I wish there was another way but there isn't. All my other saving ideas involve unarmed combat and avalanches and forest fires. I'm not very good at those things because you don't get much chance to practise them in a hole.

So I'm going to use something I am good at.

A story.

When I find the secret police, I'm going to hand myself in. Then I'm going to tell them a story about how Gabriek is a brilliant Jew-hunter who's been after me for months, on my trail, tracking me. How I can't take it any more and I want to surrender.

It's not true of course, but I'm hoping Nazis like those sorts of stories. I'm hoping they'll forgive an escaped Polish slave worker once they know he's been tirelessly hunting down a Jew.

I think they will. Two years ago I heard a Nazi say that a dead Jew is worth ten dead slave workers.

I'm pretty sure Gabriek will understand what I'm doing. It's the story game we play together in the barn, where I start telling a story and he thinks up the next part.

Gabriek's a clever storyteller, which is just as well because his part of the story will be really important.

He has to tell the Nazis that he wants to finish the job and shoot me himself. That he needs to take me to another part of the forest where the ground is softer so I can dig my own grave. That the Nazis should call it a night and go home and have a hot drink by the fire and leave us to it.

So after they've gone, we can escape.

I'm fairly certain Gabriek will be able to come up with that part of the story. I hope so, because if he doesn't . . .

What's that?

Lights through the trees, down that slope.

Torches.

Please, Richmal Crompton, if that's the Nazi hurting place, don't let me be too late.

I slither through the undergrowth until I can see down the slope.

Oh no.

Down there, gleaming in the moonlight, is a railway line running over a huge wooden bridge. The secret police are all standing around Gabriek, who's kneeling with his head close to the ground and his arms across the train tracks.

That is horrible.

I can see exactly what's happening.

The Nazis and their assistants have killed so many people in this war, they've got bored with doing it the normal way and they're trying to find new ways to do it for entertainment. Like making someone lie on a railway track so a train will chop their arms off.

And I can hear a train. In the distance. Getting closer.

I have to rescue Gabriek now.

But I hesitate.

There's a chance the Nazis won't wait for Gabriek's part of the story. There's a chance they'll just listen to my part, then shoot me themselves.

It's a chance I have to take.

The way I see it, I don't know for sure what happens after we die, but whatever happens to me will also be what happened to Mum and Dad.

So in a way, if I die, I'll be with them.

And Zelda.

Which makes me feel not quite so scared. As long as the shooting is quick. And as long as Gabriek doesn't have to see it because he's suffered enough grief already.

For a moment I don't move. I imagine Mum and Dad with their arms round me.

Then I stand up and run down the slope.

'Don't,' I yell at the secret police. 'Don't hurt him. I surrender.'

After I started yelling, the secret police all turned and pointed their guns at me, and for a moment I thought they were going to kill me before I could get my story out.

'Don't shoot,' I pant as I stumble down the slope towards them. 'I've got something important to tell you.'

My blanket gets stuck on a branch so I wriggle out of it and stagger on, keeping my hands in the air so the secret police can see I'm not ambushing, I'm surrendering.

'Felix,' yells Gabriek. 'No.'

He's on his feet and running towards me.

I'm terrified we'll both get shot now, which would totally ruin my plan.

'I give in,' I say to him loudly. 'You've won. You've worn me down. You're just too good at Jew-hunting.'

Gabriek, looking puzzled, grabs me by the shoulders.

'Back up the hill,' he says. 'Fast.'

He half-drags, half-carries me up the slope away from the railway line. There's no gunfire. Are we escaping already? That would be the best plan of all.

Then I see that the secret police are scurrying up the slope as well.

Not chasing us, running with us.

Now I'm even more puzzled than Gabriek.

'Down,' says Gabriek, pulling me onto the ground. 'Keep your head down.'

The secret police dive onto the ground and keep their heads down too. They lift them only enough to peer at the railway track.

The train is very close, the *czuk-czuk* of the engine getting louder. The last time I heard this sound, me and Zelda were escaping from a train that was transporting Jewish people to a Nazi death camp.

I have a wild thought.

Are the secret police going to stop the train and put me and Gabriek on it?

If they are, why are they lying on their tummies up here with us?

I open my mouth to ask Gabriek what's going on.

Before I can, I'm suddenly rolling over and over in a roaring explosion of wind and grit and bits of branches.

I huddle till it's finished, then rub my eyes and squint around and find my glasses.

Gabriek and the others are on their feet.

Down the slope, things are broken. Lots of the trees, and the train. A carriage is on its side, part of it hanging over the edge of the bridge.

The rest of the train, including the engine, is gone. So is half the bridge. Smoke and steam and dust are billowing up from the deep valley below.

'Stay here,' says Gabriek to me. 'Don't look.'

I think that's what he says. My ears are still stunned.

So is the rest of me. Gabriek is holding a gun.

He hates guns. We both do. Guns are what Nazis point at innocent people's heads and pull the trigger. Gabriek doesn't even like hunting rabbits with a gun. If the traps are empty he'd rather we both just eat pickled cabbage.

The other men are running down the slope shooting at the train. So is the woman with the red headscarf.

Gabriek joins them.

Nazi soldiers are trying to scramble out through the windows of the broken carriage. Before they can, they go all floppy.

Oh.

Gabriek and the others keep shooting them even after they've stopped moving. The woman in the red scarf jumps up onto the side of the broken carriage and shoots in through the spaces where the windows used to be.

Mum would never do that.

I don't want to look, but I can't stop.

I'm not stunned any more. I can tell I'm not because I'm learning new things and Gabriek always says that's the sign of an active brain.

One thing I'm learning is that these people with Gabriek probably aren't secret police. Polish secret police don't shoot Nazis, not even a little bit, and these people are doing it a lot.

The other thing I'm learning I wish I wasn't.

It's that Gabriek isn't just good at mending, he's also good at killing.

I'm hungry and I want to get back to my hole, but there's a problem. The people who probably aren't secret police won't let us go.

They're standing in a huddle on the forest path and I can tell they're talking about me and Gabriek because they keep giving us scowling looks. Even the woman with the red headscarf is, though she did just throw me my blanket.

'What's happening?' I whisper to Gabriek.

'These people are partisans,' he says. 'They live in the forests and fight the Nazis. They have to stay secret and hidden, so they're very suspicious of outsiders.'

I think about this.

'If they're suspicious of outsiders,' I say, 'why did they bring you here with them?'

'I'm not an outsider,' says Gabriek. 'They make me help them sometimes. You're the outsider.'

Gabriek doesn't say that in an unkind way, but

I can tell he wishes I wasn't here. I wish I wasn't too. I wish I was back in my hole like normal.

Except it won't ever be the same. Every night from now on, when Gabriek should be pickling cabbage or asleep in bed, I'll be wondering if he's out helping people blow up trains.

'What do the partisans do to outsiders?' I say.

'Don't ask,' says Gabriek.

One of the partisans, who I think must be the leader because he's the only one not loaded down with Nazi guns, comes over to us.

He stares at me as if he's making a difficult decision. I get the feeling he's a man who has to make a lot of difficult decisions. Such as killing a kid who might not be able to keep his mouth shut.

'I can keep my mouth shut,' I say to him.

The leader's expression doesn't change.

I feel sick.

The leader looks at Gabriek.

'Don't let it happen again,' he says.

He walks away.

Gabriek doesn't move for a moment. Just breathes.

Then he grabs my arm and pulls me in the opposite direction along the forest path.

We're hurrying through the dark forest and I'm still waiting for Gabriek to say something.

I'm also trying to get used to what I've learned about him. How he's not just a mending person, but also a shooting person and a blowing-up person and a killing person. I don't like it, but I think I understand.

The Nazis killed Genia, who Gabriek loved most in the world. So even though good people don't usually break things, I think he should be allowed to for a while. But not for too long because it's dangerous.

Gabriek still isn't saying anything, so I decide to.

'I'm sorry,' I say.

Gabriek looks at me. As far as I can tell in the darkness, his face is tired and worried and cross all at once.

I don't blame him. All parents must feel that way sometimes, specially volunteer parents.

'I thought it was a simple rule,' says Gabriek. 'You never leave the barn.'

I nod. It is a simple rule. And a good one.

I don't normally make excuses. I lived for four years in a Catholic orphanage, and one thing you learn with nuns is not to make excuses.

But I can't bear for Gabriek to think I'm stupid or careless or ungrateful.

So I try to explain why I left the barn.

Explaining is taking longer than I thought.

I keep getting out of breath. Gabriek is making us walk through the forest as fast as my painful legs can go because he says the place will be crawling with Nazis soon.

Finally I finish talking.

Gabriek doesn't say anything for a while.

When he speaks, his voice is kind of husky.

'So that's why you yelled those things,' he says.

'It was a story,' I say. 'So they wouldn't hurt you. I pretended you were good at Jew-hunting so they wouldn't know you're actually very good at Jew-protecting.'

Gabriek breathes for a while before he speaks.

'If they were the secret police,' he says, 'they'd have killed you.'

I don't say anything. Gabriek is looking even more tired and worried and cross, and I don't want to make it worse.

I can see the edge of the forest coming up. Just some fields and we'll be home.

Gabriek stops and puts his hands on my shoulders.

'Thank you,' he says.

His voice is even more husky now, but it also sounds grateful.

'I'm sorry I broke the rule,' I say. 'I won't break it again. Not unless there's another emergency.'

Gabriek thinks about this. He opens his mouth to say something, then closes it and thinks some more.

'Let's agree something,' he says after a bit. 'Let's agree we'll both do our very best to stay alive, OK?'

I nod.

'Happy birthday, Felix,' he says.

We give each other a hug. We don't often do that, but this feels like a special occasion.

I should feel happy, but as we walk towards the edge of the forest, there's a thought I can't stop having. I can't stop wishing that just for this special night the war would stop and I could have a real birthday with a cake like I used to have with Mum and Dad.

A cake with real candles.

Gabriek gives my shoulder a squeeze.

'I made you some turnip bread,' he says.

That's incredible. He must have read my mind.

We step out of the trees into the fields. And for an even more incredible moment I think my dream has come true. Over on the horizon, in the direction of the farm, flames are flickering like candles on a huge turnip cake.

But it's not a cake.

It's the farm, burning.

After staring for a few stunned moments, me and Gabriek started running across the fields towards the burning farmhouse.

Tripping over cabbage stumps.

Stumbling and frantic.

I pray to Richmal Crompton that the fire began in the house and hasn't spread to the barn yet. Hasn't spread to Dom.

Gabriek stops and grabs me.

'Stay here,' he says. 'If the Nazis did this, they might still be around. Wait here and hide in a ditch.'

Before I can say anything, Gabriek runs on towards the farm.

I hesitate, but only for a moment. Hiding in a ditch won't help Dom. And Gabriek can't put that fire out by himself. They need me.

As I stumble on, urging my stiff legs to move faster, I think about what Gabriek just said about the Nazis burning the farm.

I don't get it.

Even if the Nazis already know about their train being at the bottom of a valley all blown up and broken, how would they know we were involved?

Unless an informer told them about Gabriek helping the partisans . . .

What's that noise?

It sounds like a truck engine.

For a moment I hope it's the local fire truck. Then I remember what Gabriek told me recently. The Nazis have sent our local fire truck to the east to help repel the Russians, who've decided they don't like the Nazis and are fighting them.

I drop to the ground and crouch low and try to see whose truck this is.

Gabriek is doing the same up ahead in the next field.

There's the truck, revving its engine in swirls of smoke in front of the farmhouse. It's a Nazi truck. I can see Nazi soldiers clambering into the back.

The smoke is getting thicker. I can't see if the barn is burning or not.

Hang on, Dom.

We can't do anything while those soldiers are there. I wish Gabriek hadn't given his gun back to the partisans. I wish he could take careful aim and kill those Nazi soldiers one by one.

But he can't.

All we can do is wait while the truck drives away. And pray that while it's turning out of the farm gate it gets a puncture and rolls over and squashes those Nazi firebugs.

But it doesn't. It just drives off.

Gabriek is on his feet again and running towards the farm.

So am I.

Gabriek gets there before me.

I'm half a field back, but I can see how bad the fire is now. Flames after flames after flames. I don't think we'll be able to get water onto that many flames from just one well with a small bucket.

Gabriek has taken off his jacket. He holds it up in front of his face and goes into the farmhouse, which is burning all over.

The barn is burning too, but not as badly.

Why didn't Gabriek get Dom first?

Unless Dom is already . . . no, I don't want to think that.

Gabriek must have gone into the house because there are things inside that are even more precious to him than a really strong and loyal workhorse.

Genia things.

I'm almost at the last fence.

I beg Richmal Crompton to give Gabriek and Dom the strength to survive the heat and the smoke.

Me too.

I clamber over the fence and sprint as fast as I can to the pig trough. The ice in the trough has melted and I plunge my blanket into the water, then wrap it round my head and go into the barn.

The smoke is thick but I can hear Dom. He's making noises I've never heard him make before. Screaming noises, and noises that sound like gunshots. He must be stamping his feet.

Which isn't good. If he stamps too hard and the wooden floor of his stall gives way he'll be down in my hole and I'll never get him out.

'Dom,' I call. 'It's all right. I'm here.'

The flames are close, but only on one side. I turn my back to them and force myself towards the stall.

Dom's gate is latched with a special security latch Gabriek invented. Dom is a very smart horse and we were worried he might work out how to open a normal latch.

I know how to open this one, but not when the metal is this hot. I wrap the wet blanket round my hands, but that makes me too clumsy.

The smoke is choking us both. Dom is stamping really hard now. I grab Gabriek's axe and smash the latch off the gate. Gabriek is right, sometimes you do have to break things.

'Come on, Dom,' I say gently, putting the blanket over his head.

I keep the axe ready in case any burning beams block the way, and lead Dom out of the barn and over to the pig trough.

There's probably a taste of old pig in the water, but Dom drinks without complaining.

I peer around the farmyard.

The flames are so bright I have to squint. The heat is making the metal frames of my glasses burn my face.

I can't see Gabriek. He must still be getting things.

'I'll be back soon,' I say to Dom.

I wrap the blanket round my head again and go back into the barn. I feel guilty about not going to help Gabriek, but the flames will be in the hole soon and Gabriek's not the only one with things he wants to save.

I hold my breath all the way over to Dom's stall. My lungs are almost bursting. I open the trapdoor and drop down into the hole.

My eyes are raw and weeping from the smoke and I have to close them, but I don't need to see because down here I know where everything is.

I grab my books and my important pieces of paper and the locket Zelda gave me two birthdays ago.

The air down here is a bit fresher and I take a deep breath.

'Thanks,' I whisper to the hole. 'Thanks for the good protection.'

I climb out.

My legs hurt as usual. So does everything else because the flames are very close now.

I stagger through them to the barn door and make it outside.

Gabriek is in the farmyard. He's staring as if he can't understand how Dom got to the pig trough.

I go over to explain.

I don't get far, just a few steps.

Suddenly there's a noise as loud as an exploding train. Part of the farmhouse starts to collapse. I stagger back just in time.

'Gabriek,' I yell.

I peer through the swirling ash and sparks. The farmhouse walls are still standing, but pieces of burning roof are all over the ground.

I can't see Gabriek anywhere. Then I spot his jacket, lying on the cobbles. It's on fire. Gabriek is lying next to it.

I rush over.

His eyes are closed. For a moment I think he's dead. But he groans. He's clutching two things tightly to his chest. His violin case and the picture frame he made from one of Genia's necklaces and some of her old turnip knives.

'Gabriek,' I say frantically. 'Are you hurt?'

It's a silly question. I can see he is.

A smiling photo of Genia is in the frame. Her eyes are worried like they often were.

I'm glad she's not really here.

If she saw Gabriek like this she'd be even more worried.

You know how when the most precious living person in your life is hit by a roof and judging by the blood on him he's got a badly injured head and possibly injured hands too and you need to get him to a doctor but he can't walk and he's too big to carry so you have the idea of hoisting him up onto the back of a family member who's a strong and loyal horse?

How do you do that?

I've been trying to help Gabriek climb up, but he keeps fainting.

Wait a minute.

I've just had an idea from my education.

Of course.

I hurry over to the well through the heat and smoke, and pull on the rope till the bucket appears. I grab the axe and chop the bucket off the rope. I leave the rope threaded through the pulley, tie one end round Dom's shoulders and tie the other end round Gabriek's chest under his arms.

'Go, Dom,' I say, and make the noise with my mouth that Gabriek makes when he wants Dom to move.

Dom moves forward with slow powerful steps.

I see that patches of his fur are scorched, but he's not complaining.

The rope tightens through the pulley and slowly drags Gabriek onto his feet. I wrap my arms round his legs and as Dom takes a few more steps and the rope pulls some more, I heave Gabriek up onto Dom's back.

'Well done,' I pant to Dom as I undo the rope.

Now we have to get out of this farmyard before the rest of the house collapses.

Where to? Gabriek needs a doctor, but if we go to one in town the Nazis will grab us.

I don't know what to do.

Blood is dripping from Gabriek's head.

He slumps forward onto Dom's shoulders. His eyes are closed.

Help me, Richmal Crompton.

Gabriek opens his eyes and looks at me and mumbles something. At first I can't hear him because of the noise of the flames. I lean closer and he mumbles again and this time I do hear.

'Partisans,' he says.

After the barn roof finally collapsed in a distant shimmer of sparks, I didn't look back again. We just kept walking across the dark fields towards the forest and the partisans.

Slow steady trudging through the freezing night.

I'm keeping an eye out for Nazis, but mostly I'm looking up at Gabriek, who's on his tummy on Dom's back. I have to make sure he doesn't slide off. Sometimes Gabriek is unconscious, so he can't take care of that himself.

He can't hold on to his violin either, or Genia's photo, so I've put them in a sack with my things and hung it round Dom's neck.

'Push-ups,' mumbles Gabriek.

When Gabriek's not unconscious, he's confused. That must happen with head wounds.

Gabriek thinks we're in the barn doing my nightly exercises. I'm glad I tied his hands and feet together under Dom's belly. If you try to do push-ups on a horse's back, you'll definitely fall off.

'Armpits,' murmurs Gabriek.

I wish there was somewhere else we could go to instead of the partisans. When you're badly injured like Gabriek you need rest and gentle treatment, not spending time with people whose main activity is violence and killing. I think nuns would be a better idea. But the nearest nuns are miles and miles away and Gabriek needs medical help as soon as possible.

'Armpits,' says Gabriek again.

'It's all right,' I say to him. 'I've done my lice.'

It isn't true. With everything that's happened tonight, I haven't had time to do a lice hunt. But I don't feel bad about fibbing. Gabriek's already been hit in the head by his own roof, he doesn't need more stress.

'Wash,' says Gabriek.

'I'm washing,' I say. 'Brrrrr.'

I say that last bit because it's always cold, washing in the barn at night. But I'm not just pretending to be cold now, I am cold.

Gabriek has got my blanket. The flames dried it, so I put it over him because his jacket got burnt and I had to rip up half his shirt to make a bandage. At least with his head bandaged, Gabriek doesn't need his earflap hat, so I'm wearing that.

As we trudge I keep myself pressed against Dom's side to get some of his warmth. Dom doesn't mind. He can see my coat is thin and torn and too small. He's a very kind horse.

'Education,' mumbles Gabriek.

I start naming the parts of a clock. It's not easy. My teeth are jumping around all over the place with the cold.

And there are other reasons I'm shivering.

Worry, mostly.

What if bumping along on the back of a horse is making Gabriek's head wound worse? It doesn't seem to be bleeding as much, but I can't see what's happening inside.

I squint across the fields towards the forest, begging Richmal Crompton to make the partisans appear. I'm hoping that partisans get a lot of head wounds, so they'll know how to fix them.

Come on, partisans, where are you?

I try not to think about my other worry.

The partisan leader told Gabriek not to let it happen again.

Me turning up.

So what will happen when I do?

Still no partisans.

We've been walking through the forest for hours. We went past the broken railway bridge ages ago. Dead Nazis were still all over the place.

You'd think those bodies would be cleared away by now. The Nazis still mustn't know what happened to their train. But if they don't know, why did they burn our farm?

Dom gives a soft sad whinny.

He must be thinking about what happened to our home too.

'Irenka,' mumbles Gabriek.

Poor Gabriek has been unconscious for ages. I didn't want to wake him up in case head wounds heal more quickly when you're unconscious. But now he's awake I've got something urgent to ask him because I don't know how much longer I can stay awake myself.

'Gabriek,' I say. 'Where do the partisans live exactly?'

He doesn't reply. His eyes don't even open.

I ask him again.

'Irenka,' he says again.

His voice is croaky with sadness. And my insides go heavy with sadness too, because I realise who he's talking about. He told me once how he and Genia had planned to have a child of their own. And how if it was a girl they were going to call her Irenka after Genia's mother.

I don't know what to say.

Dom takes us on through the dark forest. The moon is behind clouds now, and even my very good night vision is having trouble making out the path ahead.

'I'm sorry,' I say to Gabriek quietly. 'I'm sorry you had me and Zelda instead of your own daughter.'

Gabriek doesn't reply.

The forest is silent except for the sound of my

soft footsteps and Dom's heavy ones. And another sound. A sound I know.

The safety catch on a gun.

'Stop right there,' says a harsh voice.

I make Dom stop.

The moon comes out again. Men are standing all around us. Men with guns, but not uniforms.

At last.

Partisans.

One of the men steps forward, his rifle pointing at us. He's very tall and thin and his bony face looks like he hasn't smiled for years. I don't blame him. The only people who smile a lot these days are Nazis.

The man takes a close look at Gabriek, who is unconscious again.

He prods me in the chest with his gun.

It hurts.

'Nazi spy?' he says.

'No,' I say, shocked. 'We hate Nazis.'

The man's expression doesn't change.

I don't recognise him. I don't think he was there when the train was blown up. I look at the other men. Most of them are standing in shadows and I don't recognise them either.

The tall partisan obviously doesn't recognise Gabriek. I need to let him know we're on his side.

'My name's Felix Salinger,' I say. 'I'm Jewish. This is Gabriek. He helps partisans. He's been looking after me and he's wounded and we need your help.'

Normally I wouldn't mention I'm Jewish, but now these partisans will definitely know I'm not a Nazi spy.

One of the other men steps forward and points at Gabriek.

'That's Borowski,' he says to the tall partisan. 'He's been on missions with Pavel.'

Pavel. That's the name of the partisan leader we're looking for. Gabriek told me that as we were leaving the farm.

The tall partisan isn't even looking at Gabriek. He's still staring at me, and his mouth looks like he's just bitten into a bad turnip.

'Jewish,' he says.

I nod.

'Jam tarts, you Jews,' he says. 'Ginger snaps. Sticky sugar mice.'

I don't know what he means, but his voice doesn't sound friendly.

'Wherever you Jews are,' says the tall partisan, 'Nazi wasps come buzzing.'

He raises his gun and points it at my head.

'Not good,' he says. 'We don't want Nazi wasps buzzing around here.'

I see his finger tightening on the trigger. Frantically I try to think of something to say. That wasps hibernate in winter?

Suddenly a sound shrills through the forest.

A bell.

Out of the darkness two bicycles are speeding

towards us. Riding them are two figures with guns slung across their backs.

The bicycles skid to a stop next to us.

Dom takes a step back.

I stare.

On one of the bicycles is Mr Pavel, the partisan leader I met before. On the other is the woman with the red headscarf, her hand still on her bicycle bell.

'Back off, Szulk,' says Mr Pavel.

The tall partisan scowls. He lowers his gun. He looks like he's been told to back off by Mr Pavel before. He also looks like he's blaming the woman for bringing Mr Pavel here.

Mr Pavel leans his bike against a tree, comes over to Dom, pulls back the blanket and peers at Gabriek's wounds.

'There was a fire,' I say. 'A roof hit Gabriek on the head. He needs expert medical help.'

Mr Pavel signals to a couple of the partisans. They come over and put an empty ammunition belt round Dom's shoulders as a kind of harness and lead him away with Gabriek still on his back.

I start to follow, but Mr Pavel grabs me.

I try to wriggle free.

'Please,' I say desperately. 'Let me help look after Gabriek. I've had experience. I was the assistant to a dentist once in the ghetto.'

Mr Pavel doesn't look like he believes me.

'His name was Barney,' I say.

I know that doesn't sound very convincing,

specially as I don't know Barney's other name. Plus, as Mr Pavel grips my arm, I remember I shouldn't be drawing attention to myself.

'Dom hasn't had any dinner,' I say.

'Don't worry,' says the woman in the red scarf. 'We've got straw. And a surgeon. If Gabriek can be fixed, Zajak will fix him.'

I feel weak with relief.

Mr Pavel lets go of me.

For a second I hope he hasn't recognised me. But he has. He's got the same weary expression he had the first time I met him.

'Get lost,' he says.

I stare at him, horrified.

He wants me to go?

To leave Gabriek and Dom?

I'm not the only one who hates this idea. The tall partisan grabs Mr Pavel by the shoulder.

'Are you crazy, Pavel?' he says 'He'll be informing on us before the Nazis get the first fingernail off him.'

Mr Pavel looks long and hard at the tall partisan, who scowls again, but takes his hand off Mr Pavel's shoulder.

I'm desperately trying to think of something to say so they'll let me stay. But before I can, the woman in the red scarf speaks again.

'We need recruits,' she says to Mr Pavel.

'He's a kid,' sneers the tall partisan.

'I'm thirteen,' I say.

I don't actually want to be a recruit. I just want to stay with Gabriek and Dom. But I keep quiet. I can see partisans are more interested in recruits than guests.

My Pavel looks at me again.

I can't tell if thirteen is old enough or not. It should be. Gabriek told me about an army in ancient Greece that was led into battle by a thirteen-year-old. They lost, but still.

'It was my birthday yesterday,' I say.

Mr Pavel is looking like he wishes he'd never met me.

'We agreed age doesn't matter,' says the woman to Mr Pavel. 'As long as a recruit has what it takes.'

'I know the rule, Yuli,' says Mr Pavel crossly. 'I made the rule. You don't have to tell me the rule.'

He looks at me again, then nods.

'All right,' he says.

He turns and gets on his bike and rides away in the same direction Dom and Gabriek were taken.

I look at the woman.

'Thank you,' I say. 'I'll be a good recruit.'

'There's a rule,' she says.

'I'm good at obeying rules,' I say. 'I used to live with nuns.'

'The rule,' says the woman, 'is that before a new recruit is allowed to join us, he or she must make a contribution.'

My insides sink.

'I haven't got any money,' I say.

Some of the other partisans snigger. The tall one doesn't.

'You don't need money,' says the woman.

'What do I need?' I say.

The tall partisan steps towards me with an unfriendly smile. He taps me on the nose with his rifle barrel.

'A gun,' he says.

After I saw that the partisans meant it, that they weren't joking, that a new recruit has to have a gun to join them, I went to get one.

Nervously.

Not sure how.

Not even sure if I want to be a partisan. Except I have to if it's the only way I can stay with Gabriek.

The woman in the red headscarf comes with me, wheeling her bike along the forest path.

'I'm Felix,' I say, to make conversation.

'I'm Yuli,' she says.

She's speaking Polish, but with a strong accent from somewhere else.

Before I can ask her where, she stops.

'That's your best bet there,' she says, pointing through the trees.

I clean my glasses on my coat.

We're on a ridge in a different part of the forest. Daylight is creeping up on us, and in the distance

I can see a grey misty town. I know it's not the town closest to Gabriek's farm because we're a long way from there.

'Good luck,' says Yuli, and gets on her bike.

'Aren't you coming with me?' I say.

She shakes her head.

'My orders are to bring you this far,' she says.

I want to plead with her to come with me. I don't know how to get a gun by myself. But I can tell from her face that partisans are as strict about orders as they are about rules.

I'm shivering, partly from cold and partly because I'm scared.

Yuli looks at me for a moment.

'You really are just a kid, aren't you?' she says.

'I'm thirteen,' I say indignantly.

I'm tempted to point out that she's only a few years older than me, but I don't. I'm tired and I need to save my energy. I've been walking all night. Early morning is nearly my bedtime.

Yuli leans her bike against a tree and takes off her gun and her leather jacket. Underneath she's wearing several layers of clothes. She pulls a wool shirt off over her head and throws it to me.

'Thank you,' I say.

'Aren't you going to put it on?' she says.

I am, but for the moment I'm staring. Her headscarf came off with the shirt. Her head is shaved. Her blonde hair is so short it's almost like dandelion fluff.

The only women I've seen with shaved heads are Jewish women after the Nazis have captured them.

I probably shouldn't ask, but I can't stop myself.

'Are you –?'

'Lice,' she says. 'They like long hair so I don't give them the chance.'

She puts her scarf and jacket and gun back on.

I put her shirt on under my coat.

Yuli is pointing to the town again.

'Plenty of guns down there,' she says.

I peer through the trees and feel another jolt of fear.

'Do you know where exactly?' I say.

'Farmers,' she says. 'Shopkeepers. Black market collaborators trying to protect their thieving hides. Failing that you'll always find a gun attached to a Nazi soldier.'

I try to look confident.

I don't feel it, but I don't want Yuli to decide this early that I'm too pathetic to join the partisans.

She's looking at me again. Her eyes are very dark for someone with blonde hair, and sort of gentle. They make her face look a bit less tough.

'Do you know how to look after yourself?' she says.

'Yes,' I say. 'Gabriek has been looking after me for a couple of years, but that's only because I had to stay hidden. Normally I'm good at cooking and washing and mending. And when I'm not having leg cramps, I can trim my own toenails.'

'I mean do you know how to fight,' says Yuli.

I hesitate. I haven't actually fought anybody since I was in the Catholic orphanage, and mostly all we did then was hard pushing.

Yuli takes my hand and puts my fingers under her chin.

'Feel the jawbone?' she says.

I nod. I'm too surprised to actually speak.

'Feel the soft part behind the jawbone?'

I nod again.

'That's where you attack,' she says. 'Doesn't matter what weapon you've got, go for that spot.'

She picks up a dry stick and snaps it in half. The ends are jagged, but blunt.

'Doesn't have to be a very sharp weapon,' she says. 'If you stab hard enough, you'll usually kill in that spot.'

I try to look like I'm grateful for the advice, but actually I'm feeling weak and a bit dizzy at the thought of stabbing someone with a stick.

Yuli gets back on her bicycle.

'Good luck, Felix,' she says. 'A lot of good luck.'

Just for a moment her voice wobbles. Not as much as my insides, but a bit.

She rides off.

I sit on a log to try to pull myself together. As well as everything else, I've just been a whole night without food.

As I sit, I smell something.

It's Yuli's shirt. The smell is quite strong, but

46

sort of familiar. I think maybe Mum smelled a bit like this. I can't be sure, but maybe.

A sound startles me.

Yuli's bicycle bell.

I look up. Yuli has stopped and is looking back at me.

'You can do it, Felix,' she calls. 'I know you can.'

She rides away.

I'm grateful to Yuli for saying that. It helps me pull myself together. Gives me courage to do what I have to do.

As I stand up, I feel something in the pocket of my coat. It's the birthday present Gabriek left for me in Dom's stall. The one wrapped in his hanky. I completely forgot about it.

I unwrap it. I put Gabriek's hanky and the string carefully back into my pocket, then I open the small box. Inside is what looks like a brass watch without a strap. Quite a big watch, with only a few scratches on the glass.

But it's not a watch. It's a compass. I can tell because it's got the first letters of north, south, east and west on it. The little metal needle is pointing to the north, the same direction as the town.

I'm puzzled. Why would you give a compass to a person who lives in a hole?

Did Gabriek know that sooner or later the Nazis would burn down the farm and I'd be roaming in a forest with no signposts? Even Gabriek couldn't know something like that, surely.

There's something about this birthday present that doesn't feel right. But I haven't got time to worry about it now.

I've got to come up with a plan.

The sooner I get a gun, the sooner I can be with Gabriek and Dom.

After I came out of the forest, I started to get nervous again.

The town was bigger than it looked from a distance. Street after street of stone houses, all with an upstairs, except for the bombed ones.

I look around anxiously.

Bigger towns have more Nazi soldiers.

I try to be positive. Bigger towns have more guns too. And the more guns there are, the better chance I have of getting one.

I hope.

So far I haven't seen anybody. People must still be sleeping. They probably think there's not much point getting up early in winter. It just uses more firewood and disturbs horses if they're asleep in the same room.

I walk along a street, trying as hard as I can not to look Jewish. That's the good thing about winter. You can wear a hat with earflaps and people don't think you're just trying to hide your face.

I've got a plan.

When I see smoke coming out of a chimney, I'll knock at the house and ask if they have anything that needs mending. I'll explain I'm very good at repairing hydraulic valve systems in hand-operated water pumps. And all types of clocks except cuckoo ones. And boots that need extra pieces of leather sewn into them for people whose feet have grown. And lamps. I'm good at mending lamps because I can work in the dark.

After I've fixed their stuff I'll tell the people not to worry about giving me money, I'd rather have an old broken gun if they've got one.

Money's scarce in wartime but there are plenty of guns around, so I think they'll prefer that. And I think I can teach myself to mend a gun.

I hope I can.

What's that noise?

It's coming from the far end of the street.

It sounds like a crowd of people murmuring. And some louder voices shouting.

I remember those sounds.

In our town when I was little, those were the sounds of market day.

Maybe this town isn't asleep after all. Maybe it's market day here and everybody's up early to grab the bargains.

A market would be a better place for my plan. If I see somebody buying a new clock or new boots, I can offer to save them money and mend their old ones.

I'd better go and see.

Oh.

It's not a market.

A big crowd of people are gathered in the market square, but they're not here to buy or sell. They're here to look.

They don't want to look. It's a horrible sight. But Nazi soldiers are everywhere, making them look. If people hide their eyes, the Nazis scream at them and they have to uncover their eyes and keep looking at the big wooden posts in the middle of the square.

And at the dead people hanging from the posts.

I don't want to look either.

But I do, because the Nazis mustn't notice me.

I stare and try not to think of Zelda and Genia. I struggle not to. But it's no good, I can't help it. I am thinking of them.

I blink a lot. If the Nazis see me crying, they'll get suspicious. They'll think I'm sympathising with the people on the posts. And disagreeing with the signs on the people.

Traitor, some of the signs say. *I Betrayed Hitler,* say others. *I Helped The Enemy,* say quite a lot.

The Nazi soldiers are glaring at the crowd.

I duck my head and slip in among other people so I won't stand out.

'Serves them right,' says a man next to me. He's

scowling at the dead people and looks almost as angry as the Nazis. 'They deserve it for helping those partisan bandits.'

I know I should keep quiet, but I can't.

People who stand up to the Nazis aren't bandits. Mum and Dad and Barney and Zelda and Genia weren't for a start.

'Partisans aren't bandits,' I say to the man.

He looks at me like I'm an idiot.

'Of course they are,' he says. 'They're all thieves and murderers and Jews.'

I struggle to stay quiet. My head is thumping with crossness and tiredness. I'm tempted to tell the man he's the idiot.

But I don't say anything. The Nazi soldiers are watching. I remember how often I had to persuade Zelda not to start an argument in front of Nazis. You couldn't blame her, she was only little. I'm old enough to control myself. I take a deep breath and force myself to look like I agree with the idiot man.

The Nazi soldiers are staring at the crowd even more closely now. They're looking for more traitors, but they'll jump at the chance to kill a Jew if they find one.

Time to get out of here.

I hurry to the outskirts of the town.

On the way I think up a new plan. The old plan won't work. Not when people are being hung in the town square for helping partisans. Even if I tell people I need a gun for rabbit hunting, they'll still be suspicious because I could be planning to make a rabbit stew for the partisans.

I need to carry out the new plan quickly, before people get back to their houses. Breaking into a house and stealing a gun isn't something I like the idea of, but I'm desperate.

This lane looks like a good one. The houses are behind trees so I won't be seen so easily, and there's a field next to the lane with rabbit holes, so some of these houses will probably have guns.

I crouch behind a clump of bushes next to a ditch and try to decide which house to break into first.

Before I can choose, I hear footsteps.

Lots of them.

And voices shouting in German. It sounds like a gang of Nazi soldiers marching down the lane.

I jump into the ditch and wriggle into a drain. It's wet and smelly and very cold in here, but I can't be seen.

The footsteps are very close now.

Except now they're this close, most of them don't sound like the thud thud of Nazi boots. Most of them sound more like shuffling.

I peek out of the drain.

And wish I hadn't.

It's an awful sight.

Jewish people, hundreds of them, thin and pale and ill, are struggling to walk along the lane while Nazi soldiers prod them and hit them.

The poor Jewish people must be freezing. Their clothes are in tatters. The biggest piece of clothing some of them have on is the patch of cloth the Nazis make them wear with the Jewish star on it.

I wish they had horses with them. Horses like Dom they could flop onto and snuggle into.

But they don't.

They just have each other to lean on.

Which isn't enough for some of them. Like that man who's just fallen down.

A Nazi soldier walks over to where he's lying and shoots him.

Oh.

Other Nazis are whipping people to keep them moving.

I know where these poor people are going. I saw a sight like this once before with Zelda and Genia.

They're going to a Nazi death camp.

Like Mum and Dad did.

I wish I had a gun. I wish I'd already broken in and stolen one so I could use it on these Nazis now. Starting with the vermin one who shot that man.

The Nazis have gone.

Just as well. If I'd spent much longer in this drain listening to what they were doing, I'd have done something berserk and violent myself.

That's the thing about spending time in small spaces. You go into your imagination and think about how the people you love have suffered.

Like I'm doing again now.

Stop it. Get out of the drain.

Except I can hear more footsteps. Just one person. But this time definitely marching.

I peek out.

Shiny boots.

Nazi vermin shiny boots. They all wear them. The one who killed the Jewish man earlier had them. And I bet the ones who killed Mum and Dad had them too. And the ones who killed Zelda, and Barney, and Genia.

As the boots get closer I squeeze myself as small as I can in the drain. But I can't squeeze away the feelings those boots are making me have.

I start to get leg cramp. I let the pain get worse, to blot out the feelings.

But the feelings just get bigger. They feel like they're going to explode.

From down here I can only see the shiny murdering boots. I can't see the actual vermin Nazi soldier, so I can't see his actual gun, but I know there'll be one.

I want it.

I listen carefully. No other footsteps coming down the lane.

Just me and him.

I peek further out of the drain.

The soldier has marched out of sight, but I know he's not far ahead. I can still hear him. And I can see what I'm looking for. Next to the ditch.

A stick.

I slide out of the drain, not caring about the pain in my legs, and grab the stick.

I snap it in half. Good, it's strong and dry.

The ends are jagged, but blunt.

Doesn't matter. Yuli showed me the spot. If you stab hard enough you'll usually kill in that spot, that's what she said.

I still can't see the Nazi soldier, but I can hear his boots crunching on the path near one of the houses.

There are trees between us, which will help me creep closer.

No, creeping isn't the way.

Running is the way. Running at him as fast as my legs will go and stabbing him as hard as I can.

He'll be bigger than me but that's good. I can get under his chin without any fuss.

I pause for a moment and think of Mum and Dad, ill and in pain and stumbling towards a death camp.

This is for both of you.

And you, Zelda.

And you, Barney.

And you, Genia.

I grip the stick tight and run full-pelt between the trees towards the crunching boots.

And stop.

And stare.

It's a boy.

He isn't much older than me. He's wearing shiny boots and a whole Nazi uniform, but he doesn't even have a gun.

Just a bike.

Confused, I duck behind a tree.

I realise what he must be. A Hitler Youth boy.

He hasn't seen me. He's leaning his bike against the wall of a house.

The door of the house opens and a man and a woman come out. The woman hugs the boy. The man gives him a Nazi salute and the boy gives him one back.

They look like proud parents.

The boy takes his boots off and the three of them go inside and shut the door.

I'm hot with sweat. Partly because of what I was going to do, and partly because of what I can see on the bike.

The things strapped to the front mudguard, one on each side. They look like explosive shells on the end of long sticks.

I think I know what they are. I read about them in the newspaper. They're special weapons for blowing up tanks. I think they're called bazookas.

I don't hesitate.

I walk over and get on the bike.

Then I get off again and crouch down and pull my boots off. I put the Nazi ones on. They're a bit big, but much better than my old ones that leak where I sewed in the extra bits of leather.

I jump on the bike and pedal as fast as I can down the lane.

I haven't ridden a bike for seven years and pedalling makes my legs hurt, but I don't care. As I speed up, the cold air stings my face.

It feels good.

I've got a bike and two bazookas.

I'm wearing boots that killers wear.

The partisans will have to think that's better than a gun any day.

After two partisans on lookout duty in the forest saw me riding towards them and took aim at me and I said don't shoot and explained I was bringing Mr Pavel something better than a gun, they took me to the partisan camp.

Well, almost to it.

I think the camp is close because I can hear Dom snorting in the distance.

I stand where I'm told, next to some bushes.

One of the partisans stays with me, holding the bike with the bazookas on it. He doesn't say anything, just keeps staring at the bazookas. I think he likes them because he gives me a smile.

The other partisan seemed to like them too before he left, so I think Mr Pavel probably will.

The partisan with me is scratching himself a lot.

'If you've got lice,' I say, 'you should really do a lice hunt each night.'

The partisan slaps me round the head.

Luckily the earflap of Gabriek's hat absorbs most of the pain. I pick my glasses up.

I think I'm meant to keep quiet.

So I do. I'm learning that obeying orders is important if you want to be a partisan.

The other lookout partisan comes back. Mr Pavel is with him.

Mr Pavel looks grumpy and sleepy. He rubs his eyes and blows his nose by pressing one nostril and snorting. He's an even louder snorter than Dom.

I wait for Mr Pavel to see the bazookas.

He does. He stares at them without saying anything, glances at me, nods to the guards, then turns and goes back the way he came.

The guard who slapped me does it again, on the back this time, so hard I almost fall over.

'Congratulations,' he says. 'You're a partisan.'

The camp isn't far, but at first I don't see it even when I'm standing in it.

I do see Dom, who's tethered to a tree with the ammunition belt harness.

'Dom,' I call happily.

'Sshhh,' hisses the partisan who slapped me. 'People are sleeping.'

We're in a clearing in the forest. I look around. It's bright daylight, but I can't see anybody sleeping. I look up into the trees. Nothing.

Then I smell something, just a whiff. It reminds

me of how I smell sometimes when the barn is too cold and I have to go a few days without a wash.

I see where the smell is coming from. A flap has opened in what looks like a grassy slope, except now I can see it's a kind of bunker built into the ground with dirt and grass all over it.

The partisan who recognised Gabriek last night is coming out, stretching and yawning and scratching himself.

I go over to him.

'Excuse me,' I say. 'Where's Gabriek? Gabriek Borowski?'

The partisan blinks at me.

I think he recognises me because his face falls.

'They just took him to Zajak the surgeon,' he says. 'Emergency operation.'

I try to stay calm. When I get stressed I get leg cramps and then I'm no good to anybody.

The partisan is hesitating from saying any more. But he's already shown me what I need to know by glancing across to the other side of the clearing. There's another grassy slope, a smaller one, which must be another bunker.

I head towards it.

The partisan follows and grabs my arm.

'Don't go in there,' he says.

I pull my arm away and run to Gabriek.

When I climb down into the bunker, I almost faint.
So much blood.

At first I think they're torturing Gabriek.

Two partisans are holding him down on a table. I can't see exactly what's going on because the door flap closes behind me and the only light is coming from candles.

A third man, who must be Doctor Zajak, is bending over doing something to Gabriek's head. Oh.

There's a hole in Gabriek's head. Doctor Zajak is doing something in the hole with a long thin knife.

I feel sick and panicky.

Gabriek looks like he's unconscious. I hope he is. But the two partisans are pressing down on his arms and legs like they think he could wake up at any moment.

'Salt,' snaps Doctor Zajak.

I realise he's talking to me.

I look around the bunker for some salt.

The bunker is small and bare, and I can't see salt anywhere.

'Salt's finished,' says one of the partisans.

Doctor Zajak swears under his breath.

He grabs a bottle of liquid and tips some on a rag he's holding, which is already wet with blood. The liquid smells like the homemade vodka Gabriek likes to drink.

Doctor Zajak wipes around the edges of the hole in Gabriek's head with the rag.

He throws the rag to me. Startled, I catch it.

'Clean,' he barks.

I can't see any clean rags in the bunker, or anywhere to wash this one.

'Quick,' shouts Doctor Zajak.

I take my hat and coat off, and Yuli's shirt. Underneath I'm wearing a wool vest and a cotton vest as well.

'Wool or cotton?' I say to Doctor Zajak.

The two partisans scowl at me.

'This isn't a shop,' one of them mutters.

'Cotton,' says Doctor Zajak without looking up.

I take both vests off and hand Doctor Zajak the cotton one. He takes it silently.

He tips vodka onto it and wipes around the edge of Gabriek's wound again. I guess because surgeons are important and save people's lives, they don't ever have to say thank you.

I can't stop looking at Gabriek's head and the blood. I wish I could stop looking, but I can't.

I pray to Richmal Crompton that Doctor Zajak can save Gabriek's life.

'Hot,' snaps Doctor Zajak.

He's holding the long thin knife out to me. I think he wants me to heat it. In a candle flame, I guess.

I take the knife and wrap the metal handle in my wool vest and hold the tip of the knife in one of the candle flames.

When it starts to glow red I hand it back to Doctor Zajak, who doesn't want the wool vest. His hands must be very tough.

There's a hissing sound. Doctor Zajak is touching

something inside Gabriek's head with the hot knife.

I smell cooking meat and feel sick again.

Gabriek starts to shudder and kick. His eyes are still closed, but he's shuddering so violently the men are struggling to hold him on the table.

'Tongue,' barks Doctor Zajak. 'Don't let him bite his tongue.'

I don't know what to do. I've never stopped anyone biting their tongue before.

Doctor Zajak grabs my hand, forces Gabriek's mouth wide open and wedges my hand between Gabriek's teeth.

Ow.

Gabriek is biting my hand. It hurts a lot, but I leave my hand there while Doctor Zajak does more things to Gabriek's head. Gradually Gabriek's shuddering stops. The biting doesn't.

To take my mind off the pain, and how cold my bare chest is, I concentrate on being helpful.

'Is there anything else you need?' I say to Doctor Zajak.

'No,' he says. 'We're finished.'

'Now,' says one of the other men, 'we pray.'

You know how when you're lying in an underground bunker and partisans are asleep all around you and the smell is worse than anything you've ever smelled including your own private parts but you don't care because next to you is a family member who's just had his life saved by an operation

64

except he doesn't seem to be breathing very much and there's a lot of blood on his bandages?

That's how it is for me and Gabriek.

I want to wake him up and tell him to breathe more. But I'm not sure if I should. When you've just had something mended inside your head, you probably need as much sleep as you can get.

'How is he?'

Somebody kneels next to me in the gloom.

It's Yuli.

She puts her gun down on the straw, takes off her headscarf and looks closely at Gabriek.

'I'm worried,' I whisper. 'I don't think Gabriek is breathing enough.'

I'm whispering because I was warned that if I make a noise and wake the partisans, they'll kill me. I think the person who said that wasn't joking.

'We just have to wait,' says Yuli. 'It's out of our hands now.'

'I know,' I say. 'It's in Richmal Crompton's hands.'

I don't think Yuli knows exactly who Richmal Crompton is.

I explain to her.

Yuli listens carefully, then tells me about some of the authors she used to read when she was growing up in Russia. They don't sound as good as Richmal Crompton, but interesting.

We talk about other things too.

Yuli tells me how the Nazis kidnapped her and made her into a slave worker like Gabriek, but she never met him in Germany because the Nazis made millions of other people into slave workers too, so it was very crowded.

She tells me the Nazis killed her parents and afterwards she changed her name to Yuli, which was her father's name, so he wouldn't be forgotten.

I ask her why she didn't choose her mother's name instead.

She doesn't answer.

The sadness on her face makes me think there are some things she wants to forget.

I tell her the Nazis took my parents to a death camp and killed them too.

We don't say much after that.

I wake up.

The smell in the bunker is just as bad and the snoring from the partisans is just as loud, but one thing has changed.

Gabriek's eyes are open.

Yuli is sitting next to him and they're talking softly.

I don't say anything. I don't want to interrupt them. I stay quietly lying down, watching them.

They seem to like each other.

That's good. Maybe they'll become friends. Maybe they'll even fall in love. If they do, maybe they'll let me stay with them.

OK, my imagination's getting carried away, but you can't help imagining that sort of thing when you know you'll never see your real parents again.

I know it won't happen.

Gabriek still loves Genia, even though all he's got left of her is her photo. And Yuli has probably got a boyfriend back in Russia. And one of the men in Doctor Zajak's bunker told me that partisans aren't allowed to get married. They get shot if they do.

Which is a shame.

Because if Gabriek and Yuli did want to be my new parents, I'd like that.

I think Mum and Dad would too.

After a long sleep, I woke up and had a stretch and something didn't feel right.

I had another stretch.

Still not right.

No dirt under my fingernails.

Then I remember where I am. With a jolt of alarm I roll over to see if Gabriek is all right.

No Gabriek.

Another partisan is asleep next to me on Gabriek's patch of straw.

I clamber over the man and crawl past other sleeping partisans to the door flap and stumble outside.

It's dark.

And cold.

I look around anxiously for Gabriek. Or Yuli or Mr Pavel or somebody who can tell me where he is.

Over on the other side of the clearing I see what looks like a group of partisans standing with their heads bowed. I hurry towards them. The moon comes out and I see two of them are holding a stretcher with somebody lying on it.

Gabriek.

I try to call his name but all I can manage is a croak.

What's going on?

Why isn't Gabriek moving?

Why are the others all just standing around?

It's like a funeral or something.

'Get him out of here,' says Mr Pavel's voice.

I can hardly breathe.

And then, as I stumble frantically towards them, I hear Gabriek's voice. It's faint and wobbly, but it's definitely his.

'If that's your final word,' says Gabriek, 'I'm not going.'

'Gabriek,' I say. 'Are you all right?'

He looks up at me from the stretcher. I can tell he's weak and in pain. Something's happened to him while I was asleep.

'Don't worry,' Gabriek says. 'You're coming with me. I'm not leaving you here.'

Leave me here?

Why would he leave me here?

'You'll obey orders,' growls Mr Pavel at Gabriek. 'I'm under orders too. When a valuable technician is badly wounded, he goes to the main camp to recover. End of story.'

'I'm going with him,' I say.

Mr Pavel doesn't even look at me. He closes his eyes and breathes deeply.

'You're staying here,' he says. 'Zajak needs an assistant.'

'No,' I say. 'I'm going with Gabriek.'

Mr Pavel looks at me and even before he speaks I can see that nothing will change his mind. It's probably why he's the leader.

'You'll obey my orders,' Mr Pavel says to me quietly. 'Or I'll shoot you.'

Nobody else says anything, and I can see from their faces Mr Pavel doesn't say something like that if he doesn't mean it.

Gabriek tries to sit up, but he can't and he slumps back onto the stretcher with a groan.

Suddenly I think of something that might change Mr Pavel's mind.

I turn and run.

'Doctor Zajak,' I say, struggling in through the hospital bunker door flap. 'You've got to come and tell Mr Pavel that Gabriek doesn't have to go. That you can cure him here.'

There's only one candle burning, but I can see Doctor Zajak lying on his table with his eyes closed.

He swears under his breath and sits up.

'Negative,' he says. 'I can't cure him here.'

'You can,' I say. 'You're a really good doctor. You got that blood clot out of Gabriek's head without dropping it or anything.'

'Don't show your ignorance,' snaps Doctor Zajak, swinging his legs off the table.

'You should have more confidence,' I say wildly. 'What makes the doctor at the main camp better than you?'

Doctor Zajak's shoulders slump and he reminds me of a nun I used to know who was always going on about what an unfair place the world is.

'Penicillin,' he says.

I don't know what that is, and I don't want to show my ignorance, but I need to convince him it's not important enough to send Gabriek away.

'We can learn how to do penicillin,' I say.

'Penicillin is a very rare medicine,' says Doctor Zajak crossly. 'Even the Nazis don't have it most of the time. The doctor at the main camp is Russian and he has a little. Your friend Borowski's wound is infected. Without penicillin, he will die.'

I don't know what to say.

Yes I do.

'Tell them you don't want me as your assistant,' I say. 'So I can go too.'

'Negative,' says Doctor Zajak. 'I do want you as my assistant.'

'Why?' I shout, close to tears. 'Why do you want me if I've got ignorance?'

'Because you've also got something else,' says Doctor Zajak. 'Experience. Yes, only with a teeth-puller, but in the forest I take what I can get.'

I stare at Doctor Zajak. I don't know what to

say. I wish I hadn't mentioned Barney to Mr Pavel. I wish I'd kept my mouth shut.

Doctor Zajak grabs one of my hands. The one he used to stop Gabriek biting his own tongue. He holds my fingers out next to his.

'Also,' he says, 'you've got surgeon's hands.'

I glare at him. That's stupid. Doctor Zajak's fingers are long and slim and leathery. Mine are short and ordinary and soft. Plus surgeon's hands don't have bright red teeth marks on them.

Yuli asks Mr Pavel to give me and Gabriek a few private moments to say goodbye.

Mr Pavel agrees.

They put Gabriek's stretcher down in a patch of moonlight and move away.

I try not to be upset. I don't want Gabriek to worry about me. Not till his head has healed.

Gabriek's voice is almost a whisper.

'Remember what we agreed?' he says. 'To do our best to stay alive. That's why I have to go. It'll be a waste if I stay here and die, after you put so much effort into saving me.'

He looks so grateful I want to tell him to stop. He saved my life every day for two years and two months.

'That's why I want to come with you,' I say. 'To look after you.'

'You'll be safer here,' says Gabriek. 'At the main camp they'd send you into combat.'

I'm about to say I wouldn't mind, but Gabriek looks at me pleadingly.

I'm shocked.

I've never seen Gabriek look pleading before. It makes me think how stressful it must have been for him these last two years, worrying about my safety.

Gabriek signals to somebody standing near us. It's Yuli. She comes over. She's holding Gabriek's violin and photo frame.

'Will you look after these for me, Felix?' says Gabriek. 'Just for a while.'

I nod. I know this is Gabriek's way of saying he'll be back.

'How long is a while?' I say.

'A month,' says Gabriek. 'Doctor Zajak says I should be fine in a month.'

I think about this.

'The main camp,' I say. 'Where is it?'

I hope Gabriek knows this is my way of saying that no way am I staying here without him for a whole month and that I'll be escaping with Dom as soon as I can and coming to the main camp.

'It's about six hours to the north,' says Yuli.

Good. Me and Dom can probably do it in five.

'It's very well hidden,' says Yuli.

I glance at her and get the feeling this is her way of saying don't bother, you'll never find it.

Well, she's wrong. I give my birthday compass a secret squeeze in my pocket.

I notice something else.

The photo frame Yuli's holding is empty. The necklace and turnip knives are still around the edges, but Genia's photo is gone. I hope we didn't lose it on the way here.

'Felix,' Gabriek says. 'I'm going to be fine. I want you to concentrate on looking after yourself. That means obeying orders.'

I nod. I'm nodding to the bit about looking after myself, not the bit about obeying orders.

Mr Pavel comes over and gives the order for Gabriek to be taken to the main camp. Two partisans pick up the stretcher. Four other partisans are travelling with them as guards.

Me and Gabriek hug each other. There's a crackling sound. I see Gabriek has got Genia's photo inside his shirt.

They start to go.

'Thanks for the birthday present,' I say to Gabriek.

He raises himself on the stretcher and looks back at me over his shoulder.

'Education,' he says sternly.

Then they're gone.

I feed Dom.

The only straw around here is from the sleeping bunker and it smells horrible and probably tastes as bad.

Dom doesn't care. He hasn't had much to eat for the last two days.

He stands up and gobbles it.

'I'm glad you like it,' I whisper to him. 'You've got to stay strong and healthy for when we leave. We might have to do a lot of running.'

Dom doesn't seem worried by that.

I give him a hug. He saved my life every day for one year and nine months, ever since Gabriek bought him from a farmer who couldn't afford to feed him.

Gabriek is so clever. To stop the Nazis taking Dom, Gabriek told them he could grow them twice as many cabbages with a strong workhorse. They believed him. It was true, but Nazis don't often believe the truth.

'Beautiful horse.'

I jump.

Yuli has come up behind me. I hope she didn't hear me whispering to Dom about leaving. She's really nice, but she takes Mr Pavel's orders very seriously.

'We're lucky to have you both,' says Yuli. 'I think you'll both make good partisans.'

I don't say anything.

'Try not to fret,' she says. 'A month will pass quickly. We'll keep you busy.'

I nod and try to smile.

Yuli strokes Dom.

'What I'm saying is don't risk it,' she says quietly. 'We have guards all over this part of the forest. You wouldn't get more than a few hundred metres.'

Yuli is looking at Dom while she says this, but I'm

pretty sure she's speaking to me. She turns to me, and I can see she's not being bossy, just concerned.

'Gabriek will always know where to find you,' she says.

She points to the tree Dom is tethered to.

'This tree's hollow,' she says. 'I told Gabriek we'd leave him a note in there if we have to move camp.'

I stare at her.

'Move camp?' I say.

Yuli looks at me as if I'm showing my ignorance.

'That's why we spend half our lives doing guard duty,' she says. 'The moment the Nazis find out where we are, we move camp. If we're lucky.'

'Which is why,' says another voice, 'once you join our little gang, you don't ever leave.'

It's the tall thin unfriendly partisan.

'Szulk,' says Yuli. 'Do you mind? We're having a private conversation.'

Szulk smiles and shrugs. He doesn't look like he really understands what a private conversation is.

'I just wanted to encourage our apprentice surgeon to do the best work he can,' says Szulk. 'Because if Zajak doesn't think he's up to the job, and decides he doesn't want him, we've got another security problem, haven't we?'

I don't understand.

'Leave it, Szulk,' says Yuli.

'I'm just encouraging him,' says Szulk. 'Jews respond well to encouragement. I'm explaining to him that if he gets fired, we can't let him waltz out of here and into the arms of the Nazis. Not now he knows so much about us. I'm sure he understands. He seems quite intelligent for a Jew.'

Yuli is staring angrily at the underneath of Szulk's chin. At the soft spot behind his jawbone. Though his doesn't look particularly soft.

I know why she's angry.

Szulk is saying something really scary. That if I'm not a good medical assistant, I'll be shot.

I hope Dom hasn't worked that out. I don't think so. He's not stamping his feet or trying to bite Szulk in the soft spot.

Szulk is staring thoughtfully at Dom.

'I hope we don't have to move camp,' he says. 'Because we don't leave food behind for the Nazis to get their hands on. We either eat it or burn it.'

He strokes Dom, but not in a nice way. It's more like somebody in a butcher's shop feeling if the meat is tender.

Szulk turns and walks away.

'Don't listen to that miserable slug,' says Yuli. 'He thinks he's the only one who's lost his family.'

But I did listen to him. And everything he said makes me anxious and worried. Specially the last bit. I've seen lots of people hungry enough to eat a horse, but never a person who'd eat Dom.

After another sleep, I started my new job. Halfway through the sleep, actually.

'Wake up,' grunts a voice in my ear. 'Zajak needs you.'

I blink and grope for my glasses. A partisan is pulling me up from the straw and making a lot of noise. He doesn't seem worried about being killed by the other partisans, even though they're grumbling and swearing in their sleep.

I stagger across the clearing, my eyes watering in the cold, and clamber down into the hospital bunker.

More blood.

And lots more noise.

A partisan is lying on the table, screaming. He's holding his knee and blood is trickling between his fingers.

'Salt,' yells Doctor Zajak, pushing the man's hand away and wrapping a scarf further up the man's leg and knotting it tight.

I peer around the bunker, desperately hoping there's been a salt delivery.

I can't see one.

'Vodka,' shouts Doctor Zajak.

I see the bottle of vodka on a shelf, grab it and hand it to Doctor Zajak. Salt and vodka must help stop wounds getting infected. I asked Gabriek once why he drank so much vodka and he said it was to stop things festering inside him. I thought he just meant feelings, but perhaps he meant germs as well.

Doctor Zajak is glaring at me.

Does he need my wool vest to wipe the vodka on with?

No, he wants my cotton vest from the hook. It's cleaner than it used to be. And smaller. Doctor Zajak must have boiled it.

I hand it to him.

He cuts away the man's trouser leg and starts cleaning the man's wound. The man is still yelling.

'Quiet,' barks Doctor Zajak.

He's saying it to me. He wants me to keep the man quiet. I shudder. Will I get my hand bitten again?

No, I have another idea.

I take my coat and Yuli's shirt off, then my wool vest. I roll the vest up and push it against the yelling man's lips. He understands what I'm doing. He opens his mouth and bites on the rolled-up vest really hard and his yells are muffled.

Doctor Zajak doesn't say thank you because he's

an important surgeon who saves people's lives.

'Hot,' he snaps.

He's holding out one of his long thin knives.

I take it carefully and heat the blade in a candle flame. I don't have my wool vest to wrap around the handle, so it starts burning my hand. I try to ignore the pain. If I'm going to do this job well, I'll need tougher hands anyway.

The bunker door bursts open and two partisans stumble in. They're carrying somebody else.

The person being carried has a lot of blood on his tummy. In fact under the shreds of cloth that used to be his coat, his tummy looks like meat.

His eyes are closed and his face is very white.

The other two partisans lay him on the floor.

I feel like I might have to lie on the floor too, and not just because of the meat. I've recognised the men who've just come in, and the one on the table as well now. They were the guards who went off with Gabriek.

Was their group attacked by Nazis?

Are these the only survivors?

'What happened?' I say weakly.

'German plane,' says one of the partisans. 'Saw us on our way back. Machine-gun practice.'

That's a relief. On the way back means they'd already delivered Gabriek to the main camp.

Behind me, Doctor Zajak swears.

I give him the knife, but he isn't swearing at me, he's swearing at the white-faced partisan on the floor, particularly the partisan's meaty tummy.

Doctor Zajak pushes the knife back into my hand.

'Bullet out,' he snaps, pointing to the knee of the man on the table.

For a moment I'm not sure what Doctor Zajak means. He's crouching over the partisan on the floor, trying to rearrange the man's tummy. He looks very busy and I don't like to interrupt.

I don't need to.

Suddenly I realise what he wants me to do.

Take a bullet out of the leg of the man on the table.

For a moment I feel faint, but this isn't helping the man, so I go over to him, trying to breathe normally so my hands won't get panicked.

I'm too nervous to look at his face, so I look at his knee.

Oh.

It's mostly meat too.

I hold the vodka vest under the man's leg to try to soak up some of the blood. It doesn't do a very good job because it's wet with blood already.

I think I can see the bullet. There's a lump of something dark half-buried in the meat. I bend closer, trying to see more clearly. I wish my glasses weren't so old and cracked.

With the tip of the knife, I carefully touch the black lump.

It's hard like a bullet.

Gently I start to slide the tip of the knife behind

the lump. I try to do it without cutting into the man's leg. It's not easy. My fingers are numb with cold and I can't see properly. The closer I lean, the more these stupid glasses don't work.

The man is starting to make loud noises through the rolled-up vest.

I try a bit harder and the knife slips. It scrapes against the hard lump.

The man screams into the vest.

'Sorry,' I say. 'Sorry.'

There's more blood now, but I can still see the bullet. It's still black, but with a white part where the knife scraped it.

Wait a minute, bullets aren't white.

Bones are white.

The black lump isn't a bullet. It must be the sticking-out end of one of the man's leg bones that got broken by the bullet.

I start to panic.

I've made the pain worse for the man and I can't even tell the difference between a bone and a bullet.

'What are you doing?'

Doctor Zajak is yelling at me, furious. He snatches the knife. He holds it in the candle flame, then touches the hot tip against the man's knee meat.

There's a hiss and the smell of cooking.

The man screams into the vest.

'I told you what to do,' Doctor Zajak barks at me. 'The bullet went in and went out. So what you do is stop the bleeding.'

I open my mouth to explain it was a misunderstanding. Doctor Zajak just said bullet out. But Doctor Zajak isn't even looking at me. He's heating the knife again. He isn't asking me to do it.

I turn to the wounded partisan on the floor to see if I can help him instead.

I can't. His head is slumped on his chest and dribble is coming out of his mouth. His eyes are open. He's not breathing.

The other two partisans are squatting next to their dead comrade.

One has sagging shoulders and his head in his hands. The other is staring up at me with an angry expression. He looks like he wants to shoot somebody.

If Mr Pavel hears how hopeless I am at being a medical assistant, he might get the chance.

'Eat,' says Yuli, crouching next to me at the edge of the clearing. She holds out her spoon.

It's a big spoon and it's full of steaming stew that's got meat and porridge in it. Normally I like stew, specially when the weather's this cold, but tonight I'm too upset.

'No thanks,' I say.

Yuli sighs.

'The world's full of injustice,' she says. 'And it's full of hunger. Why suffer them both at the same time if you don't have to?'

I can see Mr Pavel and Szulk by the cooking pot

talking together and giving me frowning looks.

'I'm just not hungry,' I say to Yuli.

She gives another sigh and glares at Mr Pavel and Szulk.

I wonder if Dom could have my share.

Yuli might not like a horse licking her spoon. And the rest of the partisans definitely wouldn't, not if she put it back in the cooking pot for another helping. So I'd better not say anything. Which is a shame. Extra food would give Dom more energy later tonight when we escape.

Yuli leans over and takes my glasses off.

She holds them up in the moonlight and peers at the lenses.

'This is a nonsense,' she says. 'How can anybody be expected to do medical work with this many cracks? And with glasses from when you were ten years old? I think it's a miracle you've got this far with them.'

She gives them back to me and looks at the partisans standing around the cooking pot.

'I'd like to see any of that lot bring back a bicycle and two anti-tank rockets half-blind,' she says.

I give Yuli a grateful smile.

It's very kind of her to try to make me feel better. I wish I could tell her how much I'm going to miss her after I leave.

After the meat and porridge stew was all gone and the sky was getting light, the partisans had a few glasses of homemade vodka, then started getting ready for bed.

Cleaning their teeth with lumps of charcoal.

Stuffing special chemical rags inside their clothes to kill the lice.

Putting their guns in flour bags to stop straw getting into the firing mechanisms.

I'm feeling tired myself after a long night being barked at by Doctor Zajak. I could go to sleep now as well, but I mustn't.

Dom is waiting for me.

Escapes always work best if you get an early start, and we've got a long journey ahead of us.

'Sleep tight, Felix,' says Yuli, yawning.

She heads off towards the women's end of the sleeping bunker.

I run after her.

'Sleep tight, Yuli,' I say, and give her a hug.

I've never done that before and she looks surprised. I hope I haven't made her suspicious. It was just the thought of never seeing her again.

'Do you want some help feeding Dom?' she says.

Yuli knows the partisans are getting grumpy about me taking their sleeping straw.

'It's all right,' I say. 'Thanks.'

'See you tonight then,' she says.

I don't answer. I turn away and hurry towards Dom and pretend I didn't hear her.

I wake up. I can't understand why I'm so cold and numb.

Even my eyelids. They're frozen together. I can't open them.

You know how sometimes when you wake up, before you open your eyes, you have trouble remembering where you are?

That's happening to me.

Hang on, it's coming back. This morning at dawn, coming over to feed Dom. And waiting here with him till everyone was in the bunker so we could escape. And starting to feel tired. And lying down for a quick nap.

Oh no, I must have dozed off.

I don't know how long I've been asleep.

It could be evening. Everyone could be getting up. I could have missed my chance to get away and find Gabriek.

Tonight could be the night they shoot me.

I force my eyes open.

White.

Everything's dazzling white. My coat, the trees, the clearing, the bunkers, Dom's shoulders, the rest of the forest, everything.

Snow.

Snow has fallen while I slept here next to Dom.

He must be frozen too. The coat I made for him from pine fronds is covered with snow. I must brush it off. I stand up.

And fall over.

Dom licks my face.

That's kind of him, but it's not my face that needs warming up.

It's my feet.

I can't feel them at all.

'Friction,' barks Doctor Zajak. 'Friction is the only cure for frostbite.'

I know what friction is, Gabriek told me once. It's what makes machines slow down, and guns get hot, and feet hurt.

I'm lying on Doctor Zajak's table. He's rubbing one of my feet and Yuli is rubbing the other.

My feet are less blue than before, but they're hurting a lot. The more the blueness and numbness go, the worse the stabbing stinging pain gets.

I wish I had the wool vest to bite on.

'Unbelievable,' growls Doctor Zajak. 'Careless.

Ignorant. Falling asleep in the snow like you're on holiday. Why not stick a sign on your chest while you're at it? *Dear Nazis, partisan camp this way.*'

I don't say anything. I don't think that's a question Doctor Zajak wants an answer to.

'You're lucky Pavel and Szulk are away on a mission,' he says.

I don't look at Yuli.

She knows I'm not careless or ignorant, so she must be wondering why I stayed out in the snow.

When I can finally get my boots on, me and Yuli go out into the clearing.

Yuli still hasn't asked me what I was doing.

The sun is setting and snow is glittering all around us.

Groups of partisans are looking miserable.

'Has something happened?' I ask.

'Snow,' says Yuli.

I understand. Even tough partisans feel the cold. But it could be worse. At least the sleeping bunker is warm. Yuli told me how last year Gabriek invented a special wood stove with pipes that put the smoke into tree roots so the Nazis can't see it.

'Snow makes our missions more dangerous,' says Yuli. 'But we have to fight even harder now. The Nazis are retreating from the Russians in the east, and soon there'll be more of them in this part of Poland.'

'So we mustn't get frostbite,' I say, to show her

I completely understand Doctor Zajak's point.

'Or leave footprints,' says Yuli, pointing to the two lines of them we've left behind us in the snow all the way from the hospital bunker.

I stare at them, thinking of the footprints me and Dom would have made if we'd escaped this morning.

'*Lines of footprints in the snow*,' recites Yuli, '*show the Nazis where to go.*'

It's a good rhyme, but I think Yuli isn't just saying it because she likes poetry.

She's giving me one of her looks.

I think she knows why I stayed out in the snow.

I try to see in her face if she's planning to say anything to Mr Pavel and Szulk when they get back tomorrow.

I can't tell.

That's the trouble with people who follow orders, even if they're nice you just don't know.

'Friction,' barks Doctor Zajak. 'Friction is the only cure for frostbite.'

I nod so Doctor Zajak doesn't feel he has to say it even more times.

The partisan whose feet me and Doctor Zajak are rubbing looks like he's suffering as much pain as I was earlier today. He's banging the table with his hands and saying things that would upset most of the nuns I've met.

'More friction,' snaps Doctor Zajak.

I'm rubbing as hard as I can. This partisan's feet are rougher and lumpier than turnips. My hands are hurting. Mostly because with these stupid glasses I keep stabbing myself on his toenails.

'Food mission?' says Doctor Zajak to the partisan.

He must be trying to take the partisan's mind off the pain.

The partisan nods and explains how three of them went to liberate some potatoes from a farmer who's friendly with the Nazis. On their way back a Nazi patrol saw their tracks in the snow and they had to hide in a frozen swamp for hours.

I'm sympathetic, but I stop listening after a while.

I need to think about my own snow problem. How me and Dom can escape without leaving any footprints before Mr Pavel and Szulk get back tomorrow.

'Sweep,' barks Doctor Zajak.

He points to a broom.

I see why. Flakes of dry skin from the partisan's feet are floating down onto the bunker floor.

Wait a minute.

Yes.

I've just thought of a way.

After I finished the final preparations for our escape, I gave Dom a pat. I could tell from the gleam in his eyes and the breath steaming out of his nostrils that he knew it was time.

To go the main camp.

To find Gabriek.

'Come on,' I whisper to Dom. 'Quietly.'

I glance towards the sleeping bunker. It's daylight now and I can see the door flap is closed and no partisans are lurking in the clearing.

Please, Richmal Crompton, don't let there be many guards on lookout duty in the forest.

With a bit of luck there won't be.

Everybody's worried about frostbite. Less guards are needed because the Nazis hate frostbite too and don't like attacking in the snow.

I make the moving-off noise into Dom's ear and we head slowly into the forest.

I look at the snow behind us.

Perfect.

No footprints.

The pine fronds Dom is dragging behind him are brushing them away as we go.

It's actually the pine-frond coat I made for him. I expanded it with some extra branches and then attached it to a rope round Dom's shoulders and it's working really well.

It does leave a sort of trail, but brush-marks aren't nearly as deep as footprints and I think the wind will blow new snow over them fairly quickly.

'Good work,' I whisper to Dom, and he drags the snow brush faster.

We head north, guided by my compass.

It's not luminous like my watch, but that's not a problem. We won't need it in the dark. We'll be at the main camp by this afternoon.

If I can keep moving.

Both my vests are in the medical bunker. This coat is thin and torn and too small, and it isn't keeping any of the wind out.

I huddle against Dom for warmth.

What's that noise?

My insides sink. I know what it is.

The safety catch on a gun.

'Stop or I'll shoot,' says a familiar voice.

Szulk steps out from behind a tree. He and Mr Pavel must have got back early.

Dom and I stop.

Szulk grins at the two partisans with him.

'Maybe we'll shoot anyway,' he says to them.

'No we won't,' says one of the other partisans. 'The kid's not running and he's not armed. I'm not shooting an unarmed kid. Let Pavel do it.'

Mr Pavel looks like he will do it.

He stands in the clearing, gripping his gun, glaring angrily at Dom and the snow brush and me.

'Cunning getaway attempt,' Szulk says to him. 'That's one thing you can say about Jews, they are cunning.'

Mr Pavel doesn't look like he's impressed much by cunning people. And he looks like disobedient people don't impress him at all.

'It was my idea,' I croak. 'Not Dom's.'

'Felix,' calls a loud and alarmed voice.

It's Yuli, hurrying over to us from the sleeping bunker. As she gets closer, I see her staring at the snow brush.

'Felix,' she says angrily. 'You promised you wouldn't try out your invention without me there.'

I stare at her. I don't know what she's talking about.

Yes I do.

She's trying to give me good protection.

Mr Pavel is staring at her as well.

'Invention?' he says.

'I was explaining to Felix how snow tracks are a big problem for us,' says Yuli. 'He came up with this.'

Szulk gives a snort of disgust.

Mr Pavel isn't snorting. He's looking doubtful, but interested.

Slowly my insides unclench.

'Does it work?' says Mr Pavel to Szulk. 'Does it hide footprints?'

Szulk is having trouble saying anything.

'Yes, it does,' says one of the other partisans who caught me.

Mr Pavel looks at the snow brush again, then does something he's never done before.

Pinches my cheek, in a nice way.

'Give him some pork fat,' he says to one of the partisans. 'And oats for the horse.'

I'm breathless with relief. Dom hasn't had oats since we left the farm. Mr Pavel must be really happy with my invention. And pork fat is a very special reward. The camp supply is buried in a sack in a secret place that only Mr Pavel and a couple of others know about. Yuli says you get a frozen slice of it, salty and fatty and delicious.

While the partisan goes to get Dom's oats and my fat, Mr Pavel and some of the others get Dom to show them how the snow brush works.

I have a vision of Dom on missions. Helping the partisans creep up on Nazis and then helping them get away without leaving footprints.

Gabriek would be so proud.

Yuli grabs me. Before I can thank her for the good protection, she takes me across the clearing.

'Shame you didn't say goodbye,' she says.

I want to remind her about the hug I gave her yesterday, but I don't want to spoil it by turning it into an excuse.

'Because if you had,' says Yuli, 'I could have given you the things I got you on my mission last night.'

She takes me into a bunker I haven't been into before.

Inside I see it's a storage bunker, where food and equipment and bullets are kept.

And something else. I've heard the partisans talking about this. Wrapped-up dead bodies that can't be buried till the ground thaws.

Piled against another wall are sacks with German writing on them.

'We ambushed a Nazi supply truck,' says Yuli. 'We hoped it was carrying guns or food. But it was carrying stuff from a concentration camp.'

Yuli rummages in one of the sacks and pulls out a thick coat. She throws it to me.

I stare at it, and at the other clothes spilling out of the sack. Clothes the Nazis stole from murdered people. I don't feel good about this.

Yuli looks at me.

I think she can see what I'm feeling.

'If you were dead,' she says, 'would you mind if your coat was keeping somebody else warm? Somebody who was fighting the people who'd killed you?'

I think about this.

'No,' I say. 'I wouldn't.'

I put the coat on. It's a bit big. But really warm.

'You'll grow into it,' says Yuli. 'Unless you pull a stunt like trying to escape again.'

Her eyes flick to the wrapped-up dead bodies.

We look at each other.

'Thanks,' I say. 'I'm sorry I doubted you.'

Yuli looks puzzled.

I've started saying it now, so I have to finish.

'I was worried you might tell Mr Pavel about my escape attempt,' I mumble.

Yuli stares at me for a while before she speaks.

'A lot of people have let you down, haven't they?' she says. 'I know they didn't all mean to, but that's how it must feel.'

I nod.

'Well,' says Yuli, 'I won't.'

We look at each other. I can see she means it.

'By the way,' she says. 'A message came through from the main camp. Gabriek is doing well. He plans to be here by the end of the month.'

I try to say thank you again, but I'm feeling too emotional.

Yuli pretends not to notice.

'I got you something else,' she says.

She opens another sack. I peer into it. Inside are hundreds of pairs of glasses.

'Amputation,' barks Doctor Zajak. 'Amputation is the only cure for frostbite this bad.'

The partisan lying on the table is unconscious,

so he doesn't hear Doctor Zajak, which is probably for the best.

'Hot,' snaps Doctor Zajak, handing me a thin knife which I now know is called a scalpel.

I heat the scalpel in a candle flame.

We get to work.

Doctor Zajak uses another scalpel to slice into the skin of the man's ankle.

I use the hot one like Doctor Zajak showed me, burning the ends of the veins and arteries so they stop bleeding.

Now I've got new glasses I can see exactly what I'm doing.

Doctor Zajak picks up his saw, which has been standing in a bucket of salty water. He saws the man's ankle for a while. I think I'm going to be sick, but I remember that the partisan has got gangrene and he'll die if we don't do this.

At least we don't have to worry about the partisan waking up. The poor man has been unconscious for three days since a Nazi grenade went off near him. Doctor Zajak says it's called a coma.

We take it in turns, Doctor Zajak with the saw, me with the scalpel.

Finally the sawing is finished.

I do the last bit of burning, and then wipe the partisan's ankle stump with vodka. Now that me and Doctor Zajak have been working together for a while, there are some things I know to do without even being told.

Doctor Zajak hands me the partisan's foot so I can see what gangrene looks like up close. Black and blotchy basically, and oozy.

It's very horrible, and if today was a couple of weeks ago I'd probably be throwing up. But the Nazis don't throw up when they see horrible things. If I'm going to help defeat them I have to learn not to as well. Gabriek would understand. He'd call it good education.

I put the foot in the bits bucket.

Doctor Zajak has left some flaps of skin hanging off the end of the partisan's ankle stump, and now he's folding them over and sewing them up.

While he does, I wipe the last trickles of blood away with the vodka vest.

Doctor Zajak looks closely at the finished stump.

'Good,' he says.

I know he's saying it to me as well as the stump. I feel proud. I've never helped cut off a foot before.

Doctor Zajak turns to me.

'Thank you,' he says.

I stop my mouth from falling open.

'Help me carry him over to the sleeping bunker,' says Doctor Zajak.

While we slowly carry the partisan across the clearing, with me stumbling sometimes, I see Doctor Zajak looking at my legs. He's been doing that a bit lately.

'You've got some muscle atrophy there,' he says.

I'm not sure what to say.

'Looks pretty advanced,' says Doctor Zajak. 'You're in for a painful old age. Only one thing'll save you.'

I stare at him. For a horrible moment I think he's going to say 'amputation'.

'Exercise,' says Doctor Zajak. 'Every day. Weight-bearing exercises. And stretching. I'll show you how.'

'Thanks,' I say, relieved.

'I'll show you before dinner,' says Doctor Zajak. 'Then you can eat, or make another failed escape attempt, or do whatever you want to do.'

He gives me a look. He almost smiles, but not quite.

I smile at him.

I know exactly what I'm going to do after the exercise lesson.

Share my pork fat with Yuli.

Then have a talk to Dom. Tell him we're staying a while longer. Until Gabriek gets here at the end of the month.

After weeks of no medical mistakes, I just made one.

Today of all days. Doctor Zajak's birthday.

'Water,' snaps Doctor Zajak, 'not vodka.'

'Sorry,' I say.

We're cutting a partisan's ingrown toenails. Hot water softens them. Vodka makes them harder.

I struggle to concentrate, but I can't.

Today is the end of the month.

Gabriek said he'd be back by today, and he's not.

All month I've been trying hard not to think about him. Not letting my mind wander while I've been helping Doctor Zajak with wound repairs and bullet removals and leg amputations and toenail trims.

But today I can't help it.

'Happy birthday, Zajak,' says the partisan on the table. 'I'll drink to your birthday even if the boy's not interested.'

He grabs the bottle of vodka and takes a swig.

'I am interested,' I say. 'Happy birthday, Doctor Zajak.'

But the partisan's right. It's hard to concentrate on Doctor Zajak's birthday while I'm thinking about Gabriek.

Gabriek always keeps his word. It's one of the things that makes him such a good person. So why hasn't he kept his word now?

Doctor Zajak is looking at me. I think he wants me to drink to his birthday. But I don't drink vodka and the only water here is in the bowl I'm holding and the partisan's feet have been in that.

'Sorry,' I say to Doctor Zajak. 'Can I drink to your birthday later when I refill the water barrel?'

Doctor Zajak doesn't say anything.

He looks at me some more, and sighs.

'Listen,' he says, and his voice is gentler than I've ever heard it. 'When Borowski said he'd be back by the end of the month, he was probably forgetting there's a war on. Plans are always changing in wartime. Travel arrangements get delayed.'

'That's right,' says the partisan. 'I ordered a taxi last July and it still hasn't arrived.'

You know how when you worry too much it all builds up until you start to get stabbing pains in your chest even though you haven't actually been stabbed?

That's happening to me.

It was nice of Doctor Zajak and the partisan to try to make me feel better, but it didn't work. I'm lying here on the straw, trying to get to sleep, and my brain is buzzing like a swarm of Nazis.

I can't stop thinking of bad reasons why Gabriek hasn't come back.

What if his head wound has made him lose his memory? Or he's gone blind? Or he's got some other medical complication? I've seen it happen. Last week we took a bullet out of a partisan's neck, and the next day his eardrum burst. He was getting wax out with the tip of a bayonet, but still.

I wish Yuli was back so we could talk.

I hate these mornings when Yuli and Dom aren't back. Yuli said last night their mission would be a long one, but I still hate them being out in daylight.

Now I'm worrying about them as well.

I take a deep breath.

I tell myself a story. Sometimes stories give us hope. Specially ones that could be true.

For example, the cooking pot at the main camp could be broken and Gabriek could be mending it before he comes back here. It could be a big job if he has to scrape all the burnt stew off first.

Or the main camp partisans could have shot down a Nazi plane and asked Gabriek to use some of the bits to improve the heating system in their sleeping bunker, including making extractor fans from the propellers.

This feels better.

I can probably think of a hundred good reasons why Gabriek isn't back yet. But I don't need to. He'll be here sooner or later, and I'm starting to feel sleepy.

Except what's that shouting?

It's the middle of the day. People are asleep. Why can't those selfish oafs have some consideration?

Wait a second.

It sounds like Yuli and Dom and the others are back from their mission, and it sounds like someone's been hurt.

I scramble out of the sleeping bunker.

Oh.

Blood on the snow.

Splashes of it everywhere.

I can see why. A partisan is lying near the bunker, blood all over him. I feel for his pulse. He's dead.

Where are Yuli and Dom?

I look around frantically.

Dom is being tethered to his tree and his official partisan blanket is being thrown over him.

He looks fine.

Then I see Yuli.

Two partisans are carrying her towards the hospital bunker. Her head is lolling and she's got blood on her face.

I sprint to the hospital bunker as fast as my legs will go. I overtake Yuli, not daring to look at her, and crash in through the door flap.

'Hot,' I yell. 'Clean.'

Doctor Zajak sits up sleepily, stares at me crossly for a moment, then swings his legs off the table as the door flap crashes open again and the partisans carry Yuli in.

'Hot,' snaps Doctor Zajak. 'Clean.'

Once Yuli is laid out on the table, I check her vital signs like I've been taught.

She's breathing.

And speaking.

'Outnumbered,' she mumbles. 'Jumped us.'

She's also bleeding. But not from her face. From her shoulder.

'Bullet wound,' I yell. 'Right shoulder.'

I feel Doctor Zajak's exasperated breath on my neck.

'Thank you,' he says. 'But if you check my vital signs too, you'll find they're all fine. Specially my eyesight.'

'Clean wound,' I say. 'Bullet out.'

I know Doctor Zajak can see that too, but I have to keep doing medical things so I don't cry.

I press the vodka cloth onto Yuli's shoulder and we check her over for other wounds. There's a lot of blood on her clothes, which must have come from her shoulder because she doesn't seem to have any other bullet holes.

But when Doctor Zajak pushes up her clothes to make sure her tummy's all right, we see something else.

Scars.

Old ones.

Bigger scars than I've ever seen, all coming from the middle of her tummy like a big star.

Doctor Zajak makes a whistling sound that I've never heard him make before, and he's seen some very serious wounds.

'Incredible,' he says. 'If she was able to survive that, she's not going to be bothered by a simple shoulder wound.'

Doctor Zajak is wrong, Yuli is bothered by it.

I can tell by the way she winces with pain whenever she moves in her sleep. Sometimes she pulls at the bandage as if she wants to take it off.

I watch her carefully in case I have to stop her doing that.

'Felix.'

Yuli opens her eyes and looks at me.

'Felix, you have to get some sleep.'

She pats the straw next to her with her good hand.

'Do your leg exercises,' she says. 'Then go to bed.'

I put Doctor Zajak's thermometer into the corner of Yuli's mouth.

When I check it, she doesn't have a fever. Which is strange because she must be delirious, thinking that a medical assistant would even consider going to sleep on duty, specially up the women's end of the bunker.

I hope she's not developing complications.

'How do you feel?' I ask her.

'Muscle wounds are always painful,' she says. 'But the worst thing is how long they take to mend. What did Zajak say, three weeks?'

I nod.

Doctor Zajak said something else about muscle wounds, but not when Yuli could hear. He said how with a muscle wound, you never know till it heals if the arm can ever be fully used again.

I look at Yuli's unhappy face and I wonder if she did hear.

I wish there was something I could do. If only we had some of that penicillin stuff.

'Yuli,' I say. 'You know how they've got special medicine at the main camp? Why don't I take you there? Me and Dom. I'll get a cart.'

She smiles at me.

'That's a sweet offer,' she says. 'But I'd rather be here where I belong. Being looked after by two top medical experts.'

It's a kind thing to say, but she's exaggerating. The top medical expert is whoever mended her tummy.

I don't say that.

'Thanks,' I mumble.

'Anyway,' says Yuli. 'You'd only be disappointed.'

I'm not sure what she means.

'Why?' I say. 'Has the main camp run out of penicillin?'

'Gabriek isn't there,' says Yuli.

I stare at her.

'I saw him last night on my mission,' she says. 'He's fine. He volunteered to join a sabotage unit. He's heading north to blow up some trains.'

I don't understand. Heading north?

'He asked me to give you a message,' says Yuli. 'To tell you he'll come here as soon as he's not needed there.'

I try to make sense of this. I want to say he's needed here too. He's needed for sabotage missions here. Me and Dom need him here.

I keep quiet.

Yuli is looking tired and in pain and I don't want to load my sadness onto her. Plus if I say anything, I'll have to say everything.

Tell her the awful thought that's been nagging at me all day like a distant air-raid siren.

I flop down onto the straw. I take my compass out of my pocket and stare at it.

Maybe this is why Gabriek gave it to me. Maybe he's had enough of the risk and danger of looking after me. Of the years of stress trying to keep a Jewish kid alive in a world full of Nazis.

Maybe he's decided he doesn't want me around any more, and I have to find my own way.

After four more weeks passed and the end of March arrived all damp and muddy and gloomy, I finally accepted the truth.

Gabriek won't be coming back.

Ever.

I know he could if he wanted to. If he told the partisan leaders he wanted to do his missions from this camp, he'd be allowed to because he's the best. The partisan leaders would let him come here to keep him happy. People do their best work when they're happy, it's a medical fact.

'People who blow up trains,' I say to Doctor Zajak, 'they do their best work when they're happy, don't they?'

Doctor Zajak gives me an uncertain look.

But he nods.

Then he puts his arm round my shoulder.

'Or angry, Felix,' he says quietly. 'Some people do their best work when they're angry.'

I go outside and squat down next to the pit where we bury the things we amputate.

I think about this.

Doctor Zajak's right. Some people definitely do their best work when they're angry. Look at Adolf Hitler. He's angry all the time and he's the most successful mass-murderer ever.

I've been so dumb. Just a feeble-minded kid who thought he could solve any problem by telling himself a cheerful story.

What an idiot.

Cooking pots. Gabriek hasn't spent the last two months mending cooking pots. In two months you could make a mountain of brand new cooking pots, even if all you had to work with were melted-down fillings from dead Nazis. And you could turn about ten Nazi planes into alarm clocks in two months.

I know the truth now.

The reason Gabriek's not coming back is because he doesn't want to.

'Felix,' says Yuli. 'Are you all right?'

I bury my face in the straw.

Yuli must be wondering what I'm doing here in the sleeping bunker at night. Partisans hardly ever sleep at night.

'I'm fine,' I mumble.

Normally Yuli leaves people alone with their feelings, it's one of the good things about her. But tonight is meant to be a happy night. The snow has started to melt, and Yuli's shoulder is completely healed. Earlier today she did some fast shooting practice and hit every single one of the Hitler pine cones.

'Are you thinking about Gabriek?' says Yuli softly.

I nod miserably into the straw.

'Why did he promise?' I say. 'If he didn't want to come back, he could have just said goodbye.'

Yuli puts her hand on my shoulder.

'He did want to come back,' she says. 'But things change and at the moment there are more important things he has to do.'

'Exactly,' I say bitterly.

'Felix,' says Yuli. 'Think about what I've told you. About the vital work Gabriek and the others are doing. Hurting the Nazis as they retreat from the Russians.'

I shrug. I've heard all this before. It doesn't make me feel any better.

'We've just had new information,' says Yuli. 'About how urgent that work is. We have to stop the Nazis getting back into Germany and unleashing their secret weapons.'

I roll over and look at Yuli.

'Secret weapons?' I say.

'There are all sorts of rumours,' says Yuli. 'Fighter planes that fly faster than sound. Atomic bombs more powerful than a thousand volcanoes. And they're not all rumours. The Nazis have already started launching giant rocket bombs at England.

Rocket bombs that fly themselves.'

I stare at her.

England is where Richmal Crompton lives.

Nobody I care about is safe from the Nazis. They've made Gabriek so stressed that he doesn't want me any more, and now they're even trying to kill Richmal Crompton.

'I wish I could do vital work hurting the Nazis,' I say bitterly.

Yuli looks at me.

I see her make a decision.

'Felix,' she says. 'Would you like to come on a mission with me and Dom?'

I don't say anything. Did I hear her right?

'Tomorrow night,' says Yuli. 'To the town where you got the bazookas.'

Now I don't want to bury my head in the straw.

'Yes,' I say. 'I would.'

It's exactly the sort of cart I'd planned to get. A big wooden farm cart with strong wheels. The partisans took it from a farmer who was friendly with the Nazis.

Sitting on the seat, holding the reins while Dom pulls us along the dark forest path towards the town, me and Yuli look like a typical farmer and her son.

'Not son,' says Yuli. 'I'd have been nine when I had you. If anyone asks, we're brother and sister.'

I know she's right, but I don't care.

In my imagination she's my mum, and we're on a mission to hurt Nazis together.

I was a bit disappointed at first when I found out my first mission was only a food mission. But I'm not any more. Yuli explained that for partisans, food is as important as bullets. Every potato we bring back is another stab in the heart of the Nazis. And every turnip.

Which feels good.

This mission was her idea. It's simple and very clever, which is what you'd expect from the person who had the idea of putting Hitler moustaches on pine cones to make targets.

Instead of stealing food and risking a shooting battle, we're going to the market to buy food. The Nazis won't even know we're partisans. And we're travelling at night because real farmers always get to market very early, before dawn.

'Yuli,' I say as we creak along behind Dom. 'Where did the money come from to buy the food?'

'The same Nazi supply truck as your coat and glasses,' says Yuli. 'But it's not exactly money.'

She hands me a cloth bag.

It feels heavy. I look inside.

Jewellery.

Gold and silver and gemstones sparkling in the moonlight.

I remember that the Nazi supply truck was bringing stolen Jewish possessions from a death camp. I also remember that Mum had a silver watch that used to belong to her mum.

I start rummaging among the jewellery.

'What are you looking for?' says Yuli.

'My mum's watch,' I say.

Yuli gently takes the bag from me and closes it.

'Different camp,' she says softly. 'Your parents would have died in a camp further north.'

We don't say anything for a while. That's how it is with war, people have so much sadness to think about.

There are lots of rings in the bag. Hundreds. I can't imagine how many memories people would have had about those rings.

'Yuli,' I say. 'Do you think you'll ever get married?'

If she's planning to, she should save a ring for herself. I'm sure the person who owned it wouldn't mind.

Yuli shakes her head.

She looks sad. Maybe she's feeling the same as me about Gabriek not coming back.

'Why not?' I say. 'Why won't you ever get married?'

'It's personal,' says Yuli quietly.

'Sorry,' I say.

But Yuli tells me anyway. I think she remembers how I've told her quite a few personal things about myself.

'Last year,' she says, 'I got a lot of shrapnel in me from a Nazi grenade. I won't ever be able to have children.'

I think about that. I can understand why some

men wouldn't want to marry a woman if she couldn't have children.

But not all men.

'What if you fall in love with a man who's already got a child?' I ask. 'Even just a borrowed one?'

Yuli doesn't answer.

I understand. It's not the same.

Poor Yuli.

No wonder she wants to kill Nazis so much.

We hear the shooting just after we've been through a small village on the outskirts of the town.

Yuli steers Dom and the cart off the road and we stop under a tree.

Ahead of us the road goes down a slope, and at the bottom are the lights of a farmhouse.

A few figures with lanterns are moving around in front of the house.

I think two or three of the figures have got Nazi uniforms on.

One of them raises a gun and points it at the head of what looks like an old woman.

He shoots her.

Oh.

'Look at those scum,' mutters Yuli. 'Looting for themselves.'

I know what she means. In a history lesson with Gabriek once, I learned what retreating armies usually do. They destroy stuff so the other side can't use it, and they loot for themselves.

Of course. I should have realised.

That's probably why the Nazis burned our farm.

'Wait here,' says Yuli.

I look at her, startled. Where's she going?

She pulls something from her boot.

A knife.

I start to panic. She's going after Nazis and she hasn't even got a gun. Mr Pavel said not to bring one in case we get searched.

Too late. She's gone.

I stare down the road at the farmyard, where the Nazi soldiers look like they're drinking out of bottles.

No sign of Yuli.

To take my mind off things, I tell Dom a story. About a Russian farm horse who can't have children. She meets a Polish farm horse who already has a young donkey he looks after, and together they all rebuild his barn.

I can't finish the story. I used to like animal stories, they reminded me of my friend Zelda. But this one feels stupid.

I see Yuli.

In the farmyard.

She's got her arm round one of the Nazi soldiers, and she's drinking out of his bottle. She and the soldier are both laughing.

I don't know how she can do that, drink out of the same bottle as a Nazi.

Her arm moves really fast and the Nazi soldier

isn't laughing any more. He's on the ground, kicking his legs and clutching his throat.

Yuli spent half this afternoon sharpening her knife and now I can see why.

Look out, Yuli, the other two Nazis.

I don't have to worry. With another fast arm movement she grabs the first Nazi's gun and flames start spitting out of it.

I feel proud of her.

And I feel proud of myself too. I helped Doctor Zajak do a good job mending her shoulder, so in a way I'm helping her blow those two Nazis' brains out.

After we got to the square in the middle of the town, me and Yuli did the same as the other people who'd arrived early for the market. We stretched out in our cart under a blanket and closed our eyes. But only for a while because then the town was bombed.

Sirens screaming.

Searchlights in the dark sky.

The sound of thunder getting closer.

At first I don't know what's happening.

'Quick,' yells Yuli.

I help her steer Dom and the cart into the middle of the market square, next to the posts for hanging people. It's so that buildings can't fall on us. We get Dom to lie down, then we both lie flat too, huddled together next to him on the cobbles.

All around us other farmers are doing the same.

The first explosions shake the whole square.

I put my arm on Dom's head to try to keep him

calm. You don't get noise like this on farms, not even in a hailstorm.

The noise gets worse.

Not just explosions, the roar of breaking buildings.

A few times I hear bits of buildings whizzing over our heads. From the screams in the square I think some of them are landing nearby.

I squint up to try to see the vicious heartless Nazi planes that are killing innocent farmers and don't even care.

'Keep your head down,' yells Yuli.

Gradually the explosions stop, and the buildings aren't crashing so much, and the thunder high above us slowly goes away.

'Dom,' I croak. 'Are you all right?'

He is. So is our cart.

We peer around.

Others aren't so lucky. Dead bodies and weeping people and broken carts.

'Come on,' says Yuli. 'We have to find food.'

For a moment I want to stay and help the wounded people in the square. There might not be anybody else here with medical experience.

Then I remember we're on a mission to hurt Nazis.

This town is completely broken.

Every street has bits of buildings lying in it, and bits of people. Other people are wandering around crying. When we find food, I hope we don't have to take it from crying people.

'Those Nazi vermin pilots,' I say. 'Bombing people who aren't even in armies.'

I wish I had the bazooka rockets from the bike. I could have blasted those Nazi vermin planes out of the sky.

Yuli is giving me a look.

'That wasn't the Nazis doing the bombing,' she says. 'It was the British and the Americans.'

I stare at her.

The Americans are on our side. Doctor Zajak told me. And Britain is where Richmal Crompton lives.

'The railway junction here is a Nazi transport hub,' explains Yuli. 'And there's a Nazi regional headquarters here too. The way the British and Americans see it, with this many Nazis around, it's easier just to take out the whole town.'

I'm shocked.

I bet Richmal Crompton would be too.

Yuli grabs my arm.

'Talking of Nazi headquarters,' she says, pointing down the street.

I see what she's pointing at. A tall broken building with half a tattered Nazi flag hanging off the front.

'Wait here with Dom,' says Yuli, jumping down from the cart. 'Look for food.'

She takes off her leather jacket and headscarf

and throws them into the back of the cart. I don't know why she's doing that. It's barely daylight and it's freezing.

Now I do.

There's a dead Nazi soldier lying near us. Yuli takes his jacket and helmet, puts them on, grabs his gun and hurries towards the Nazi headquarters.

I wish I was going with her.

I'd like to help her kill some Nazis in their own regional headquarters.

I find a quiet side street that doesn't have people wandering around in a daze or lying around in bits.

There must be food in at least some of these broken buildings.

I tether Dom to what's left of a lamppost. I don't want to leave anything in the cart because one of the things about war is that people take what isn't theirs. Clothes, bikes, food, you name it. So I put Yuli's jacket on over my coat, stuff her headscarf into the pocket, and grab the bag of jewellery.

I look at the buildings.

I try to decide which is riskier. Searching for food in an upstairs flat where the floor might give way, or in a basement flat where the ceiling might collapse.

Before I can decide, I see someone move behind a bombed-out window.

I freeze.

Yuli told me that sometimes Nazi soldiers from

the local barracks kill town people and steal their apartments. What if this is a Nazi soldier? One who's popped home to see if his stolen kitchen crockery has survived the bombing?

He wouldn't expect a partisan to creep up on him. And shoot him in the head while he's inspecting his dinner plates for cracks.

I wish I had a gun. I could go and find one. Or I could go and get Yuli and we could kill the vermin Nazi together.

Slowly I back away towards the cart.

I glance at the bombed-out window again.

And see a face. A young girl. She's got dark hair and dark eyes.

I stare.

Zelda?

No, that's stupid. I saw Zelda's poor dead body myself more than two years ago.

I hear children's voices whispering, and the young girl disappears from the window as if she's been pulled away.

I can't hear any grown-ups. If there are children alone in that wrecked apartment, they must be scared. I remember how terrified Zelda was about being left alone in wartime. I know how I feel myself sometimes.

Slowly, so the children don't think I'm attacking, I go over to the building to see if I can help.

It's easy to get into the building because a large part of the front is missing. I walk into what used to be a living room, crunching on broken glass and chunks of ceiling plaster.

'Hello?' I call, trying to sound friendly.

I hear whispers coming from behind a pile of wrecked furniture.

'I am being quiet. Stop being bossy,' a young voice hisses indignantly.

Then I notice something at the back of the room. Part of the wall has broken away, and behind it is another room, a little one with no windows. On the floor of the little room are three kid-size mattresses. There's also a bowl with wees and poos in it, and a water bottle.

It's a hiding place.

I know what hiding places look like because I lived in one for two years and two months. And there's mostly only one type of kid who has to live in a hiding place in Poland in 1945.

'It's all right,' I say to the pile of wrecked furniture. 'I'm Jewish too.'

No reply.

Of course. If I was a Nazi, I'd say that, wouldn't I? To get them to come out so I could kill them.

'Amcha,' I say carefully.

It's a word Yuli taught me. It's not Russian, it's Hebrew. It's a kind of Jewish password. Nazis can use it too, but they don't know how to say it properly.

I wait.

There's more whispering and a bit of scuffling.

A girl, older than the one I saw, steps out from behind the furniture.

'Do you have any food?' she says.

Two other girls come out. One of them is the one I saw. She looks about five. The one who just spoke looks about twelve. The other one looks like she's somewhere in between.

'No,' I say. 'Sorry.'

'What's in the bag?' says the oldest girl.

'Just jewels,' I say.

'I'm hungry,' wails the youngest girl, and starts crying.

I look around the apartment.

'There must be some food in here somewhere,' I say.

I can see that the grown-ups who live here aren't poor. The smashed-up furniture has got cushions.

'The food's under the bricks with Mrs Fidetzky,' says the middle girl, looking like she's going to cry too.

The oldest one points through a doorway.

I go and look. Half the kitchen has collapsed, and sticking out from under a pile of bricks are two legs in stockings.

'Are you a looter?' says the oldest girl.

I shake my head.

'I'm a partisan,' I say.

I can see none of them know what that is. I don't bother to explain. We all need food too urgently.

'Are there any shops in this street?' I say.

The oldest girl shakes her head.

'Mr Motyl in the basement flat next door has food,' she says. 'Millions of tins of food. He's the foreman in a food factory and he steals it. Mrs Fidetzky told us.'

'We're too scared to get some,' says the middle girl. ''Cause he hates Jews.'

'Wait here,' I say. 'I'll go and see if I can persuade him to share. If he won't, my mum will have a word with him.'

The girls all look doubtful.

I don't tell them how Yuli would persuade him. Best if they don't know the details.

After I went into the street and checked that Dom was all right, I thought about the best way of persuading Mr Motyl to share his food.

Go and fetch Yuli?

I decide not to. If the Jewish girls next door are right, and Mr Motyl is a thief and a hoarder, he's probably greedy too. Maybe he'll be happy to swap some tins for some jewels. Then Yuli won't need to get involved and at least that'll be one less person killed in this town today.

But I don't get to speak to Mr Motyl.

Outside the wrecked basement flat next door, a man in overalls is lying with a big piece of wood sticking out of his chest. Next to it, on his overalls, is sewn the word Motyl.

I don't bother checking Mr Motyl's vital signs. Not with a piece of wood that big.

I go into the flat, hoping some of the tins have survived.

'Stop in the name of Adolf Hitler,' says a voice. 'Or we'll shoot.'

Normally I'd be scared if somebody yelled that. But this voice is squeaky and wobbly. And speaking Polish.

I put the jewellery bag down and raise my hands to show I'm unarmed.

A boy steps out of the gloom.

He's wearing a Hitler Youth uniform and pointing a rifle at me. The rifle is shaking. He doesn't look much older than me.

I watch his trigger finger closely. I can feel big splinters of wood under my feet, and I can clearly see the soft spot under his chin.

'What do you want?' he says.

'Food,' I say. 'I can pay.'

I touch the jewellery bag with my foot.

The boy seems uncertain what to do next. He glances over his shoulder and says something in German. Somebody else steps forward.

Another boy. I stare.

I've seen this boy somewhere before. I remember where. It's the bicycle boy. He's still wearing his Hitler Youth uniform, but it's torn and scuffed. He must have got other boots. They're scuffed too.

He scowls at me, but I can see he doesn't have a clue I'm the person who took his things.

'What makes you think we're selling?' he says. 'What makes you think we won't just take your money?'

'Because if you do,' I say, 'my mum will kill you.'

The bicycle boy sniggers.

'I'd like to see that,' he says.

'You wouldn't see it,' I say. 'She'd cut your throat before you even knew there was a knife. Haven't you heard how partisans do it?'

The bicycle boy gives a nervous snort.

'You're not a partisan,' he says. 'You haven't even got a gun.'

'I don't need a gun,' I say. 'I've got a bike and two bazookas and a new pair of boots.'

The bicycle boy looks startled. He stares at my boots, and then glances anxiously around.

'*Dummkopf*,' the first boy says to him in German. Then something like 'I told you it was partisans.'

The bicycle boy sort of sags. He doesn't look tough now. He looks like somebody's given him a beating. Which, judging by the bruises on his face, I think somebody has.

'Take as much food as you want,' he says to me sulkily in Polish. 'Won't be any use to you.'

'It's all tins,' says another voice, a girl's. 'There's no tin opener.'

The girl steps into view. She's about five, with curly hair so blonde it's almost glowing. Though that could just be my eyes getting used to the gloom.

Now, behind the three kids, I can see tins. Hundreds of them, stacked up against the walls. No labels, just gleaming metal tins.

'There must be a tin opener,' I say. 'Nobody

would have this many tins without a tin opener.'

'Dad hid it,' says the girl sadly.

'So burglars couldn't find it,' says the boy with the rifle, and for a moment he looks like he's going to be the first Hitler Youth I've ever seen cry.

I don't blame him. If that was my dad lying dead by the front door with wood in his chest, I'd be bawling my eyes out.

The boy doesn't cry. But he scowls, and sort of droops, and lowers his rifle.

On the floor I can see where they've been trying to open the tins. There are a few dented ones and some pieces of stone and wood.

'Let's do a deal,' I say. 'I'll show you how to open them and you give me half the tins.'

'Have you got a tin opener?' says the little girl hopefully.

'Sort of,' I say.

The two boys aren't looking happy, but they haven't said no.

I open the jewellery bag and give the three of them a ring each. I choose ones with big sharp diamonds.

Gabriek taught me about this. If you want to cut something hard, you need something sharp and harder. Nothing is harder than a diamond. Except perhaps a Nazi's heart.

I put a diamond ring on one of my fingers, grab a tin, make a fist and scrape the ring round and round the top of the tin in circles. It takes quite a while, but suddenly the top caves in and I can lift it off like a lid.

Meat stew runs down my arm.

The other three are all doing the same.

The bicycle boy gets his tin open first. He throws the lid away and gobbles the stew like he's starving.

I'm curious. German families living in Poland aren't usually starving.

'Why aren't you at your place?' I say. 'With your mum and dad?'

The bicycle boy looks at me miserably over the top of his tin.

'Bombed,' he mumbles.

For a fleeting moment, in my imagination, I have a horrible vision. The whole of Europe full of kids on their own. Struggling to survive the world's biggest parent shortage. Trying to find their own way.

I am so lucky to have Yuli.

I grab the jewellery bag and an armful of tins.

'I'll be back for the rest of my share,' I say to the three kids.

The boy with the rifle raises it and points it at me again. He's not droopy now, and he's scowling even more. And the rifle isn't wobbling.

'What if we don't let you take any?' he says. 'What if we're sick of being pushed around and bombed?'

'Helmut,' says the little girl indignantly. 'He's nice.'

Helmut obviously doesn't think so. His rifle is aimed at my head. Under my armful of tins, my chest is going like a machine gun.

I manage to look Helmut directly in the eyes and speak calmly.

'My mum is just up the street,' I say. 'On average she takes about five seconds to kill a person. I also work with a man who knows how to remove any part of the human body he wants, usually in a few minutes. And he hardly ever uses anaesthetic.'

Nobody speaks.

The little girl stares at me, drops of stew trembling on her bottom lip.

Helmut looks doubtful again and lowers the rifle.

I keep my voice steady.

'Like I said, I'll be back for the rest of my share.'

The bicycle boy pulls himself together.

'Yeah,' he says. 'Well you'd better bring lots of reinforcements or we might not let you in.'

I give him a contemptuous look, like the one Szulk gives me sometimes.

The little girl is watching all three of us, eyes darting from one to the other, scared.

I turn and leave.

I feel bad about scaring a little kid, but I push the feeling away. I know what Yuli would say. If you start feeling sorry for Nazis, you're dead.

When the three Jewish girls from next door see me coming out of the basement flat with the tins, they run out of their flat to meet me.

I give them a diamond ring each and show them how they work.

The oldest girl gets her tin open in record time, and gives some stew to her little sisters.

'Thanks,' she says to me.

'You're a good partisan,' says the middle girl through a mouthful of stew.

I hope she's right. I've got a difficult decision to make now.

How many tins do I give the girls, and how many do I load onto the back of the cart to feed the partisans and strike a blow into the heart of the Nazis?

Search me.

To give myself time to think about it, I decide to go and find Yuli.

I turn, and see her running towards me.

'Felix,' she yells. 'I told you to stay put.'

'You told me to look for food,' I protest.

The girls are shrinking back fearfully. I realise it's because Yuli still has the Nazi jacket on.

'It's all right,' I say to them. 'It's just dress-up.'

'Come on,' Yuli yells at me, jumping into the cart and grabbing Dom's reins. 'We have to leave. Now.'

'But I've found food,' I say, pointing to the basement flat. 'Loads of it.'

'Now,' yells Yuli.

As I get onto the cart, I look down the street to see if we're being chased by Nazis. I can't see any.

I don't get it.

'What's happened?' I say as we head off.

'We've got to get back to the forest and warn the others,' says Yuli.

'What about?' I say.

Yuli doesn't reply at first, just urges Dom to go faster.

She looks different to how I've ever seen her.

Panicked.

'I went to the headquarters to get information about Nazi troop movements,' she says. 'I got information all right. The Nazis know where our camp is. They've been planning an attack. Because of the bombing, they're doing it today.'

After we got to the forest, Yuli stopped looking behind us to see if we were being followed and instead started peering anxiously ahead.

Tense.

Listening.

For the Nazi attack.

She keeps glancing down at the forest path.

I see why. There are tyre tracks in the damp earth.

From the look on Yuli's face, I guess the tyre marks are probably from Nazi trucks.

Dom's back and shoulders are glistening with sweat in the weak cold sunlight, that's how much effort he's putting into getting us back to camp.

'Faster,' mutters Yuli to him. 'Faster.'

I do the 'faster' noise Gabriek taught me, but it doesn't make any difference. Dom is going as fast as a horse like him can.

Yuli is still wearing the dead Nazi soldier's jacket.

She's still got his gun. I wish he'd had two guns, so Yuli and me could have one each.

Then we hear it.

In the distance.

Shooting.

Yuli yanks on the reins and stops the cart. She pulls the Nazi jacket off and puts on her coat and headscarf.

'Take Dom to the swamp,' she says. 'Wait for me there.'

I stare at her.

Swamp? I don't know any swamp.

'I want to come with you,' I say. 'I want to fight the Nazis with you.'

Yuli shakes her head.

'Use your compass,' she says. 'Go south-east till you reach the swamp. Wait for me there.'

'No,' I say.

I'm going with her. She's my mum now. You don't go lazing around in swamps while your mum's fighting a huge Nazi attack.

Yuli's arm moves so fast I don't realise what's happening at first.

Then I do.

She's holding the barrel of the Nazi gun against my throat. The soft part under my chin. The part she taught me about.

'That's an order,' she says.

Her eyes are blazing and furious. They're also full of tears.

I try to speak. I try to plead with her. But my voice won't come out.

Yuli squeezes my arm so hard it hurts.

Then she jumps down from the cart and runs between the trees, out of sight, towards the shooting.

There's no forest path going to the south-east.

Dom has to drag the cart through the undergrowth, over rotten logs, his feet slipping in drifts of slimy leaves.

He's doing this for me, working hard to get me away from danger.

And I'm letting him because you don't take a horse into a gun battle if you can help it, not even a big strong horse like Dom.

Yes, I'd stay close to him and give him good protection, but if I got killed he'd be on his own.

I steer Dom between the trees, but he doesn't really need me, he can do it by himself.

Anyway I'm distracted, listening to the distant battle. Trying to tell the difference between Nazi gunfire and partisan gunfire.

I want it all to be partisan. Including big explosions as the Nazis get blasted with my bazooka rockets. I want the only Nazi sounds to be dying ones. I try to picture them all dead, so I won't have to think about Yuli in the middle of a battle with only one gun and no ammunition belt.

The cart lurches over a log and something slides against my feet.

The jewellery bag.

Yuli didn't take it. I wish she had. She could have put diamond rings on all her fingers and when her bullets ran out and her knife got blunt she could have fought on, taking the tops off Nazi heads.

I smile at the thought.

Then I stop smiling.

The jewellery bag reminds me of Mum.

What would Mum and Dad say if they saw me grinning about people having the tops of their heads removed, even Nazis?

They'd be sad and disappointed.

Mum and Dad never felt glad about somebody else's suffering, not once in their lives. Not even when a man tried to steal a big expensive book from their shop and it fell on his wife.

I push Mum and Dad's sad disappointed faces out of my imagination. I'm glad they aren't here to see the sort of person I've turned into. They'd try to understand, but they might not be able to.

I'm lucky.

Yuli is my parent now.

She understands.

You know how when you reach a forest swamp at sunset and the ground is so wet it's shimmering and you see what looks like an island way over across the water and you think what a great hiding place but you don't go there because you want Yuli to be able to find you and so instead you tell Dom a story about a brave partisan woman who marries a grumpy but fair partisan leader or maybe a grumpy but kind partisan doctor and they adopt a young partisan and his horse, and halfway through the story you realise that the distant battle sounds have stopped and you're tempted to go and see what's happened but you don't because you're under orders, so you fall asleep with Dom on the shore of the swamp and you wake up in the freezing dawn and Yuli still hasn't come?

That's just happened to me.

I stand up.

Ow.

My legs hurt. So does my back. And my neck.

I'm hungry. Dom must be too. We haven't eaten for one day and two nights.

But none of this is worrying me as much as the other thought in my sleepy brain.

The battle ended last night. That was hours ago. Loads of time for Yuli to get here.

So where is she?

I try not to panic. Instead I follow the advice Gabriek used to give me.

When you're feeling stressed, keep busy.

'Come on,' I say to Dom, wiping the cold dew off his back with my sleeve. 'Let's go and find her.'

A_{fter} we got close to the partisan camp, Dom and I stopped behind some trees so I could listen.

No gloating Nazi voices or trucks.

No wounded partisan moans of pain.

Just the drip drip of dew from the branches all around us and the distant crackle of a fire.

A fire is good. A fire means cooking and getting warm and drying clothes that are a bit sweaty after winning a battle.

I lead Dom out of the trees into the clearing.

Oh.

I put my hands over Dom's eyes so he doesn't have to see. I don't want to see either. I take Dom back into the trees and tether him so he's facing away from the horrible sight.

I want to stay facing away too, but I can't.

I force myself to turn round.

Sprawled in the clearing are partisans, blood on their clothes, their faces in the mud, not moving.

For a few moments I have to hold on to a tree. It helps a bit when I see that all the red patches are blood and not a headscarf, but only a bit because there could be other bodies out of sight.

I work my way across the clearing, going from body to body, checking for vital signs.

Nothing.

The dead partisans look like they've been shot extra times to make sure.

'Yuli,' I yell, in case she's hiding somewhere, waiting for me.

I go and look. She's not in the sleeping bunker, not even up the men's end. I don't bother looking in the storage bunker because the whole thing's on fire. Instead I run to the hospital bunker. Yuli's not in there either.

Doctor Zajak is.

He's on his table. He looks like he's just done fifty operations without time to put on a fresh apron. But the blood on his front isn't from fifty operations, it's from him.

I step closer and see the bullet holes.

Too many for hot.

Too many for clean.

Doctor Zajak's eyes are open, staring at his scalpels on the shelf. I wish he could feel proud and satisfied at the thought of all the lives he saved with them. And I wish I could thank him for all the good education he gave me.

But that's one of the worst things about war.

Everything happens too quickly. You don't get a chance to say goodbye.

Not properly.

Not to anyone.

Gently I close Doctor Zajak's eyes like he taught me. Then I hurry out of the bunker, desperately trying to think where else Yuli could be.

A thought hits me. So far I've found eleven bodies including Doctor Zajak. But there were more than eleven partisans in our group, more than twice that many.

Where are the others?

Did they get away?

I run over to the hollow tree, the one we used to tether Dom to. Yuli said if the partisans ever had to move on, she'd leave a note there.

I reach inside the tree.

Gabriek's violin is there, exactly where I left it, wrapped in a piece of oily sacking inside the violin case for safe keeping.

But no note.

Not inside the tree, or the case, or the violin.

I stand there, numb with disappointment. I can't believe Yuli would shift camp without letting me know where she was going. Even if Mr Pavel was yelling at her to get a move on she'd leave a message.

Wouldn't she?

I hear a creaking sound.

For a wild second I hope it's Yuli, hiding up a tree, making the branch creak as she climbs down.

I look around at the nearby trees.

Oh.

It's not Yuli, it's Mr Pavel.

And he's not climbing down. A rope is round his neck and his body is twisting in the breeze making the branch creak.

The Nazis like hanging people. It's their way of showing the world they can break anything they want to.

Frantically I search the other trees for more hanging bodies, but there aren't any.

So there's still a chance.

Yuli and the others might have got away.

That's what I think until I go over to the burning storage bunker, hoping a bit of food might not be burnt so me and Dom can eat it.

I smell a horrible smell.

A smell that's like burning meat but different.

I smelled it yesterday in town, after the bombing, when me and Yuli hurried past burning buildings with dead bodies in them.

The frozen bodies of dead partisans used to be stored in this bunker. But when the snow thawed, we buried them.

So why is there this smell now?

Then I see it, lying by the entrance to the bunker. It's only a fragment and it's charred round the edges, but I'd recognise that red cloth anywhere.

Yuli's headscarf.

I pick it up and stare at it and the horrible sickly

141

smell of burning bodies makes me want to throw up and also makes me want to fall down because now I know.

The others didn't get away.

None of them did.

Dom knows too.

He stands patiently, letting me hold on to him and press my face into him and make his fur wet.

In my imagination I give Yuli a last hug.

And thank her for the good protection.

And promise to tell everyone about her, so her name and her father's name won't ever be forgotten.

I can feel Dom's muscles twitching sadly. I wish I had muscles that big. So big I could kill hundreds of Nazis with my bare hands. Just smash them and rip them and break their veins and arteries.

Except what's the point?

It wouldn't bring Yuli back. Or Mum and Dad. Or Zelda or Barney or Genia or anyone.

I'd still be missing them.

Year after year after year after year.

Sometimes you don't have to actually live in a hole to feel like you're in a dark and lonely place.

Life must go on, that's what Gabriek always says.

I wipe my snot off Dom. He's not complaining, just looking at me with his gentle eyes. I can see how sad he's feeling about poor Yuli too.

He waits patiently while I bury the partisans.

The ones from the clearing, and Doctor Zajak.

It takes ages but Dom doesn't mind.

Digging helps when you're sad. It doesn't make you feel better, but it helps you think.

I wonder why the Nazis didn't burn all the partisans' bodies?

Perhaps they couldn't fit them all in the storage bunker. Perhaps their officers told them to stop wasting time being firebugs. Perhaps they just got bored.

Anyway, it's an honour for me to bury these brave partisans. Specially Doctor Zajak. It's a way of saying thank you.

And it's helped me make a big decision.

I'm not going to bother with parents any more.

Wars aren't a good time for parents. You see it everywhere. Kids upset and angry and bitter because of what's happened to parents. It's not the parents' fault, it's just the way it is.

I think in wartime you're better off doing without parents.

Look at Dom. He hasn't seen his parents for years and he doesn't spend his time moping about them.

From now on I'm not going to bother with parents either.

After the bombing started again, I knew it was safe to go back into town to get the rest of my tins of food.

That's the one good thing about bombing, it distracts Nazis.

'Try not to worry,' I say to Dom as we walk along a dark street, steering the cart between piles of rubble. 'Most of the bombs are falling on the other side of town tonight.'

That's mostly true, but sometimes there's an explosion very close, even louder than a big horse stamping on a plank of wood right next to your ear. And straight afterwards there's the creaking crashing noise of a building breaking into pieces.

The cold wind is full of gritty dust.

I'm all right, I've got glasses and Gabriek's earflap hat. I'm glad I put a blanket over Dom's head to shield his eyes.

'The straw will protect us,' I say to him.

Our cart is piled high with potatoes and oats and straw. Not stinky rancid sleeping-bunker straw. Clean fresh delicious straw. Enough to keep Dom going for weeks. If you choose the right farmer, it's amazing how much straw and oats and potatoes a bag of jewels will get you, even in wartime.

If a lump of building does fall on us, I'm hoping the straw will cushion the blow.

It's the people without straw I'm worried about. The Jewish girls in the apartment haven't got any straw. If a bomb falls on their building, all they'll have to cushion the blow is a few cushions.

'Hello,' I call out as I crunch my way into the girls' apartment. 'It's me again.'

Silence, except for the distant sound of buildings breaking.

I know I should be getting the tins from next door and hurrying away, but now that I've started thinking about the girls I want to see if they're all right.

I light one of Doctor Zajak's candles and hold it up and look around the living room. And feel a jolt of disappointment.

The little hiding-place room at the other end is empty. The three mattresses are gone.

There's much more rubble in the living room. And bits of furniture I haven't seen before. Stuff must have fallen through the big new hole in the ceiling.

'Shhhh.'

Was that a voice, or just some gas leaking in the bombed-out kitchen?

I stand very still and listen.

'It might not be him,' whispers a voice. 'It might be a trap.'

The voice sounds like the oldest girl. But it isn't coming from behind any of the piles of furniture, it's coming from under the floor.

'What's the password?' says another voice loudly. That one sounds like the middle girl.

'We don't have a password, idiot,' whispers the oldest girl's voice.

'Yes we do,' says the middle girl's voice.

I hold my candle flame close to a crack between the splintered floorboards.

From my pocket I take the ring I saved to open tins with. I push the diamond part into a crack so the girls can see it.

'*Amcha,*' I say.

There's silence, then sounds of movement.

In the corner of the room a couple of floorboards lift up and the oldest girl's head appears. She looks tired and hungry and miserable. Her skin is pale and stretched tight, which happens to very hungry people.

'You're wasting your time,' she says. 'If you've come for more tins, you shouldn't have bothered.'

'I've come to see if you want to go to another hiding place,' I say. 'A safer one.'

The girl looks at me like I've been hit in the head by a piece of sideboard from upstairs.

I haven't. I just said that without planning to. But I'm glad I did.

'There isn't a safer hiding place,' says the girl. 'The whole town's being bombed every night.'

'I know a place,' I say. 'In the forest. An island.'

The girl thinks about this. She looks partly doubtful and a bit hopeful. She climbs up into the room and helps her two younger sisters climb up.

'Is there food on the island?' she asks me.

'And coconut trees?' says the youngest girl.

I shake my head.

'I'll get more food from next door,' I say. 'More tins.'

'No you won't,' says the oldest girl. 'Next door's been hit by a bomb.'

Mr Motyl has disappeared.

Outside the entrance to the basement flat next door, there's just a huge pile of rubble. Nothing is sticking out, not even Mr Motyl's feet.

I climb over the rubble and peer into what used to be the flat.

Lots more rubble. No tins.

The tins must be buried in here somewhere. But if something can get buried, it can get unburied. Gabriek would agree with that.

I make myself stop thinking about Gabriek. There's just me now.

147

I wriggle into the flat and start digging.

It's a slow job. I have to twist round and push each piece of rubble out through the opening behind me.

Twist after twist.

Brick after brick.

I'm tempted to ask the girls to come in from the cart to help me. But there are probably things in here the younger ones shouldn't see.

Dead Hitler Youth boys, very likely.

I grab another piece of rubble. And another.

Rubble after rubble after rubble.

Then I move a chunk and something behind it glints in the light from my candle.

A tin.

I scrabble to get to it.

And hear a groan.

For a second I have a crazy thought. It's Mr Motyl, back from the dead to stop me taking his tins. But there's another groan and it comes from under my knees.

'Help,' says a muffled voice.

I claw at the rubble, flinging bricks and lumps of plaster away. Then I'm kneeling on something else.

The top of a table.

Ow.

A fork is sticking into my shin. I put it into my pocket because forks are scarce in wartime.

While I'm doing that, some of the rubble collapses, and now I can see what's under the table.

Three people, huddled and sobbing.

One is hugging his knees.

Another is hugging a rifle and his little sister.

I recognise the uniforms even under all the dust.

'Rescue us,' says the little girl.

The two Hitler Youth boys don't say anything or do anything, just stare at me. They don't look like they care who I am or what I'm here for. But I can see they want me to rescue them too.

For a few moments I don't want to rescue them. I think of Mum and Dad and Yuli and the others and I want to hurt them.

Then I remember I'm doing without parents now.

People who aren't bothering about parents shouldn't bother about revenge either.

We're nearly at the forest, which is a relief. I was worried daylight would start before we got here.

It's not Dom's fault, he's been working his hardest. It's just that the cart is so loaded. A layer of tins and a layer of straw and a layer of potatoes and oats, and on top of all that another layer of straw and a layer of kids and another huge layer of straw.

'Are we there yet?' calls a grumpy voice from under the straw.

I sigh. I knew being patient and quiet was going to be hard for the little kids, who are only about five, but I didn't think it would be this hard for the Hitler Youth boys as well.

'Almost,' I say. 'Be patient.'

'If these filthy Jews don't stay over their side,' says Helmut's voice, 'I'm chucking them out of the cart.'

'You touch my sisters,' says the oldest girl's voice, 'and you'll get this tin in your teeth.'

Helmut mutters something in German.

I sigh again.

I'm tempted to tell them that if they don't stop squabbling, they can all get out and walk.

But I don't. It's not their fault. You have to expect arguments when you've got Jews and Nazis in the same cart.

Things will be better when we get to the island. When they see we're all in this together. All sharing the same good protection.

I hope.

'**After** it's been in a Nazi's mouth?' exploded Hannah, pushing my toothbrush away. 'No chance.'

I sigh.

I struggle to stay patient.

This is our third day on the island and I thought we'd finally got the rules sorted out.

Wees and poos into the north side of the swamp, drinking water and washing water only from the south side.

No fires during the day.

No mixing up our sleeping hay and Dom's eating hay.

Leg exercises twice a day for those who have to do them, which is just me at the moment.

And no going to bed without cleaning our teeth.

Obviously we still haven't got that one sorted out. I wonder if Mr Pavel had this problem.

'I'm not sharing a toothbrush with a Nazi,' mutters Hannah.

I sigh. I was hoping an oldest sister would set a better example.

'I'd rather have rotten teeth than Jew-spit in my gob,' retorts Axel the bicycle boy.

'Stop it, both of you,' I say. 'You're lucky we've got a toothbrush.'

I've explained to them all why partisans are so strict about teeth cleaning. You can't stay in a forest with toothache. You make too much noise, plus you could get a jaw infection and die.

'OK,' I say to Axel. 'Don't clean your teeth. Your decision. And in a couple of weeks you can go back to the bombing and try to find a dentist.'

Axel glares at me, and mutters something in German, but he grabs my brush and starts cleaning his teeth.

After Axel and Helmut do theirs, and Helmut's little sister Bug does hers, I boil the brush in the potato pot and Hannah, Beryl and Faiga do theirs.

I stare at the tattered bristles. It was an old brush when Yuli gave it to me, and now it's looking even older. I wonder how much longer it'll last with seven of us using it.

Live life one day at a time, that's what Gabriek used to say when I was in the hole.

I shouldn't have done that. Started thinking about Yuli and Gabriek. If I get emotional, Axel and Helmut will think I'm going weak and they might try to take over as leader.

The truth is I'd love somebody else to take over.

But I can't risk it while they're all squabbling.

'Come on,' I say sternly. 'Bedtime.'

I get Dom to lie down on his straw. Hannah helps me lift our pine-branch sleeping shelter over him. Then we all lie down and snuggle up against Dom and each other and pull our coats over ourselves.

'I can't sleep with a Jew on my foot,' says Helmut.

I lose my temper.

'Helmut,' I say angrily. 'We've been through this. We haven't got any blankets. We need to share body warmth. You don't hear Dom complaining, and he doesn't even have to sleep lying down. He's just doing it to be kind.'

'Anyway, Helmut,' says Hannah, 'there are worse things than having a Jew on your foot.'

'Like what?' scowls Helmut.

'Well,' says Hannah, her voice suddenly icy. 'How about if you were killed in the night? By a Jew who's decided to make you Nazi pigs pay for what you did to our parents?'

There's a long silence.

Helmut and Hannah glare at each other.

I don't know how I'll get them apart if this turns violent. Axel doesn't look like he'll help.

Helmut suddenly rolls over and curls up with his back to Hannah.

'Just stay off my foot,' he growls.

Hannah gives him a last glare and rolls over with her back to him.

Slowly the others settle back down.

I take a deep breath.

In the distance, through the dusk, I can hear the faint sounds of something moving in the undergrowth.

A wild animal?

A Nazi soldier looking for our footprints in the mud?

I'm glad there's a swamp between us and whatever it is. A swamp you need a big strong horse to carry you across.

But what if the Nazis get a big strong horse?

I wish I hadn't started thinking about this.

I'll be awake half the night worrying.

How did this happen? Last week I decided to do without parents, and now I am one.

I wake suddenly.

Somebody's crying.

I assume it's one of the little girls, Bug or Faiga.

But as my eyes get used to the darkness, I see it's neither of them.

It's Axel. He's sobbing in his sleep.

The others have woken up now. Even Dom. We're all lying here, staring at Axel.

Helmut gives him a dig.

'Axel,' he hisses. He says something in German. Probably 'You're embarrassing yourself.'

Axel wakes up. He looks at us all. He shudders a bit, like you do when you've been crying. Then his eyes widen and he touches his wet cheek.

He looks horrified and embarrassed.

Helmut does the sort of snort that tries to sound like a laugh but isn't.

'Jesus, Axel,' he says. 'Keep a lid on it.'

'Keep a lid on it,' repeats Faiga, giggling. Bug starts giggling too. They're carrying on like a pair of five-year-olds. I'm about to tell them off, then I remember they are a pair of five-year-olds.

Axel's face suddenly crumples again.

'Why?' he says. 'Why should I keep a lid on it? My parents are dead. My whole family's dead. Our house has gone, my school's gone, I couldn't even bury my dog because our garden's gone.'

He runs out of breath.

Snot and tears are dripping from his face.

Nobody moves. Nobody's giggling now.

We just lie silently.

I see tears on Hannah's cheeks too.

I stand in the grey dawn. I pee into the swamp and do what every parent does at the start of a new day.

Worry about food.

We've been on this island for two weeks. We've eaten more than half the tins and potatoes. And Dom has eaten most of his oats and hay.

I finish my pee, but I don't go back to the sleeping shelter because this is serious and I have to think.

If we can't get more food, we'll have to leave here in another two weeks and our good protection will be over. Three weeks at the most if we eat less and share some of the tins with Dom.

But how can we get more food? I spent the rest of the jewellery on the potatoes, oats and hay.

Which means all we can do is try to steal food and risk being caught by the Nazis.

'Felix,' says a sad little voice.

Faiga is wandering towards me, rubbing her eyes. Hannah's coat is round her shoulders and dragging behind her in the wet grass.

'I'm sad,' says Faiga.

I crouch down and pull the coat more warmly around her.

'I miss my mummy and daddy,' she says.

'I know,' I say gently.

'Mummy and Daddy were shot in a forest,' says Faiga. 'Hannah said so. Will we be shot in a forest?'

I put my arms around her.

'No,' I say. 'We won't.'

It's what a parent has to say. You can't say 'I hope not', or 'who knows', or 'if this war goes on for many more years we might'.

It's one of the hard things about being a parent.

I don't know how they do it without getting sad and scared themselves.

'You don't know anything, you idiot.'

Faiga and I haven't even got back to the sleeping shelter yet, but I can already hear the others squabbling.

This is hopeless.

'I do know things,' says Hannah's voice. 'I know you haven't even got any bullets.'

'That's where you're wrong,' says Axel's voice. 'I've got plenty.'

'Five,' says Helmut's voice.

I can see the whole group now through the trees. Sitting under the sleeping shelter having their own private war as usual.

'Guns are stupid,' says Beryl.

'Boys are stupid,' says Bug.

'Not as much as girls,' says Helmut.

I stare at them.

Did they just say what I thought they said?

At last. It's what I've been hoping for. No more Nazis against Jews. Just girls against boys.

'What's the problem?' I say as I walk over with Faiga.

'We're bored,' says Hannah.

'If we have to sit on this dumb island with dumb girls much longer,' says Axel, 'our bums'll grow roots.'

Faiga laughs.

Beryl glares at her and she stops.

'We're sick of hiding away like this,' says Hannah. 'We want to fight the Nazis.'

I look nervously at Axel and Helmut.

Helmut is sitting on his own, scowling. But Axel is nodding too. Did he hear what Hannah just said?

Now I'm confused.

Axel sees me looking puzzled.

'We didn't want to be Nazis,' he says. 'They made us because our parents were German.'

He looks like he means it.

'And you'd fight them?' I say. 'You'd fight against the Nazis?'

'They ruined everything,' says Axel. 'That vermin Adolf Hitler has ruined my life.'

'Axel,' hisses Helmut.

The two German boys glare at each other.

'Hitler's ruined your life too,' Axel says angrily to Helmut.

Helmut looks like he's going to argue.

But instead he droops.

'Yeah,' he mumbles.

His little sister goes over and puts her arms round him.

'Our mum and dad were proud of Helmut in the Hitler Youth,' says Bug. 'He was keeping our family safe.'

'Didn't work, though, did it?' says Helmut sadly. 'Adolf Hitler should have stayed in Munich and been a travel agent, that's what our mum said before she died.'

We all think about this, and how different all our lives would be if he had.

'Here's what we should do,' says Hannah. 'Find poisonous mushrooms in the forest and make a soup and creep into the Nazi barracks and mix it with their food.'

'That's a dumb idea,' says Axel. 'We should ambush them and shoot them.'

'What with?' says Hannah. 'Your bullets haven't even got any gunpowder. Helmut said you dug them out of a wall.'

'That doesn't mean they haven't got gunpowder,' says Axel, hurt.

My mind is racing. Suddenly I can see a way to let the others do what they want to do and get more food at the same time.

'I've got an idea,' I say.

I explain what Yuli told me about the local railway line being a major Nazi supply route. I tell them about the Nazi secret weapons. Specially the rocket bombs that fly themselves to England.

'If we wreck a train,' I say, 'we'll be doing big damage to the Nazis. We might even stop some rocket bombs getting to the launching sites up north. And even if we don't do that, Nazi supply trains will almost certainly have food on them. We've got three Nazi uniforms between us. Three of us can salvage food from the wrecked train and blend right in.'

The others are all looking at me.

Gobsmacked.

'Wreck a train,' says Hannah. 'How do we wreck a train?'

'With a lot of explosives,' says Axel. 'Which we haven't got.'

'That's not the only way,' I say.

I glance across at Dom, who has wandered away from the squabbling to scratch his back on a tree.

Dom is looking at me.

I can see he understands.

He knows that if we're going to wreck a train, he's the most important part of the mission.

After I explained to the others that the best way to wreck a train without explosives or parents is to get a big strong horse to drag a section of track away so the train gets derailed and falls over, and they agreed it sounded like a good thing to do, we got busy with the preparations.

Days after days of preparations.

Finding the railway track.

Seeing how often trains come past at night.

Choosing a well-hidden section of the track to remove.

Working out we need a crowbar to loosen the metal clips that hold the track down.

Deciding which piece of metal we can unscrew from the cart to use as a crowbar without the cart falling to pieces.

Taking the piece of metal off.

Watching the cart fall to pieces.

Rebuilding the cart.

'Typical,' says Hannah scornfully. 'Boys always get things wrong.'

'Typical,' says Axel, just as scornfully. 'Girls always think they know best and they don't.'

'Stop it,' I say, 'or I'll cancel the whole sabotage.'

At last we're ready, so we wait for a dry night and set off.

The bigger ones walk next to the cart so Dom can save his strength for what he has to do. I don't know what a section of railway track weighs, but it must be a lot. About as much as ten ploughs probably.

I hope Dom can do it. I stroke his leg muscles as we walk. I'm a bit worried he might have caught a cold from carrying us through the swamp so many times over the last couple of weeks.

It would have been better not to bring the cart tonight, but Faiga and Bug and Beryl are too small for a long walk through a dark forest, and we couldn't leave them on the island by themselves.

Nobody is saying much.

The little kids are asleep in the back of the cart. Axel, Helmut and Hannah are walking silently. As we pass through patches of moonlight between the trees, I see how tense their faces are.

I'm feeling the same.

Trying not to think about how risky this is.

Axel and Helmut are wearing their Hitler Youth uniforms, and I'm wearing the Nazi uniform Yuli left behind, but what if the Nazis see through our disguise?

I pat my chest under the Nazi jacket to make sure my medical package is safe inside my shirt. Doctor Zajak's scalpels and needles and a candle, wrapped in my cotton vest.

If any of the others get bullets in them, I can do clean and hot, but whether that'll be enough to save them I don't know.

This is another hard thing about being a parent. Wanting to give good protection and not knowing if you can.

You know how when you reach a railway line and you're desperate to get to work removing a section of track but first you've got to unharness Dom and hide the cart carefully in thick bushes so that if Nazis start killing and hurting they won't find Faiga and Bug and Beryl?

That's what Axel and Helmut and me are doing.

We tear off pine branches and cover the cart, leaving small spaces so the little girls can breathe.

'It's like a doll's house,' says Bug.

'Let's be dolls,' says Faiga.

'Partisan dolls,' says Beryl. 'Brave ones.'

Hannah isn't helping us. She's staring at the bridge further along the railway line, and the deep valley it runs across.

'I still think we should be doing our sabotage on that bridge,' she says.

I explain to her again why that wouldn't be a good idea. How the derailed train would fall into the valley and we couldn't get the food from it.

'Also,' I say, 'Nazi train drivers are used to being sabotaged on bridges, so they pay extra attention on them. Once the train's across, the driver will relax and won't see our sabotage up ahead.'

Hannah mutters something about how more Nazis get killed when they fall into deep valleys.

She's right, but I remind her we're mostly doing this for food.

'I'm not,' she says.

'That's enough branches,' says Axel. 'Let's get started.'

'Just a few more,' I say. 'The corner of the cart is still showing.'

I bend down to pick up more branches.

Before I can get my hands on them, I'm suddenly rolling over and over in a roaring explosion of wind and grit and stinging pine needles.

The explosion echoes away through the hills.

I find my glasses and struggle to my feet.

Hannah, Axel and Helmut are picking themselves up too. The little girls are still in the cart, whimpering. Dom is still standing, but he's stamping unhappily.

I try to calm them down.

I also try to see what's happened.

Axel and Helmut and Hannah are staring down the slope, open-mouthed.

I see what they're looking at.

Clouds of dust and smoke.

The railway bridge is broken and twisted, more than half of it gone.

'It got blown up,' says Helmut.

He's right.

'Must be partisans,' I say.

But which partisans? Yuli and Mr Pavel and the others are all dead. Could it be the partisans from the main camp?

Below us, down the slope, a figure holding a gun steps out from the trees and starts walking through the dust and smoke towards the broken bridge.

I stare, my heart thumping as much as when the explosion first went off.

Gabriek?

The dust and smoke are starting to clear.

It's not Gabriek. It's a Nazi soldier.

Other Nazi soldiers come out of the trees and join the first one on what's left of the bridge.

Where are the partisans? Why aren't they shooting the Nazis?

I signal to Hannah and the others to stay crouching low and out of sight. I don't take my eyes off the Nazis.

Two of the soldiers are tying something to the part of the bridge that's still standing. A small package with a wire attached to it.

All the soldiers hurry back into the trees, trailing the wire behind them.

I realise what's going to happen.

I can hardly believe it. I whisper to the little girls to put their hands over their ears and not be scared by another loud noise, and then I put my hands over Dom's ears.

It happens.

Another explosion, a smaller one.

The rest of the bridge collapses.

Hannah and Axel and Helmut are staring, stunned.

I know exactly what they're thinking. Why are the Nazis blowing up their own bridge? I'd be thinking it myself if Gabriek hadn't given me such a good education. If he hadn't explained that retreating armies don't just do looting and destroy other people's stuff.

There's something else they do.

Remembering it now makes my insides leap.

Sometimes retreating armies destroy their own stuff as well, but only when they know they've lost the war.

Our journey back to the swamp starts off much happier than our journey earlier tonight.

When I tell the others what Gabriek said, they all get very excited.

'Does this mean the war's over?' says Beryl.

'It could be soon,' I say.

I take the Nazi jacket off and fling it away into the trees.

Everyone chatters happily about the war being over. Axel and Helmut even sing a couple of songs, which they promise aren't Nazi ones.

Gradually, though, we all go quiet.

I know why.

It's wonderful when a war ends, but then you remember that things will never be the same.

Everyone you've lost will still be dead.

Parents and relatives and pets and best friends.

And some people, even if they're not dead, you'll never see again.

I hate war and the way it makes you have so many sad thoughts, because now I can't stop thinking about Gabriek.

I can't stop thinking about how he'll be feeling after the war.

He'll be glad the Nazis are defeated, but there's something he won't be glad about. He won't be glad he ever met me and Zelda. And I can't blame him. If we hadn't arrived at his farm, Genia would still be alive.

Irenka might even be born.

We all walk on in silence.

The little girls are asleep in the cart again.

I want to sleep too as soon as we get back, so I can get rid of these horrible thoughts.

We're almost there. I can see the dawn mist rising off the swamp.

I peer ahead to find the place where we cross to the island.

And see a figure, waiting on the shore.

The mist is quite thick, but I know instantly who it is. Even when mist is this thick, you can see colours through it.

This colour is different from how it used to be, not as bright, but it's still red and it's still a headscarf.

Yuli.

After Yuli and I finished hugging, and started hugging some more, and I introduced her to the others and explained she was one of my best friends, I asked Yuli a million questions.

How she survived.

Where she went.

Why it took her so long to come back.

'I was lucky,' says Yuli sadly. 'Luckier than Pavel and most of the others.'

She tells us about the Nazi attack on the camp. How the partisans were outnumbered and overwhelmed. How she was knocked unconscious by the blast from a grenade. How when she woke up, she found herself in a different camp far away in another part of the forest.

'The main camp?' I ask.

Yuli shakes her head.

'A new camp,' she says. 'With Szulk in command.'

I pull a face, then explain to the others how

awful that must have been for Yuli.

'We had someone like that in our Hitler Youth brigade,' says Axel.

Yuli looks at him, but doesn't say anything.

She must be wondering what I'm doing hanging around with Nazis.

'Axel's on our side now,' I say to her. 'So's Helmut.'

She still seems doubtful, so I tell her how Axel and Helmut were going to help us wreck a Nazi train if the Nazis hadn't got in the way.

Yuli gives Axel and Helmut a friendly nod.

'It's happening all over,' she says. 'The Nazis are in a panic and destroying everything. There's a rumour Hitler has killed himself.'

Our cheers echo across the swamp.

Yuli stays silent. And serious.

'Felix,' she says. 'I've got some other news. Two lots. One bad, the other . . . well, not so bad. Maybe.'

I stare at her.

'Tell me the bad first,' I say.

You have to say that in wartime. There's so much bad news, it often makes the not-so-bad news pointless.

Yuli puts her arm round me.

'Doctor Zajak was killed,' she says.

'I know,' I say quietly. 'I went to the camp after the Nazis had gone.'

Yuli stares at me.

'Was it you who buried the bodies?' she asks.

I nod.

She keeps staring at me. It feels really nice, but I'm embarrassed about her doing it in front of the others because they haven't got grown-ups to look at them in an amazed and concerned and proud and loving way.

'What's the other news?' I say.

Yuli hesitates. She swallows a couple of times.

This is strange. I don't think I've ever seen Yuli hesitate about anything.

'Felix,' she says. 'This might be nothing. It's just a tiny, tiny chance.'

'What?' I say. 'What chance?'

'Your parents,' she says.

At first I'm not even sure if I'm hearing her right.

'A few weeks ago,' says Yuli, 'the Nazis closed down the camp your parents were probably taken to. They moved the survivors to Germany.'

I can hardly breathe.

'Survivors?' I say. 'How could there be survivors? It was a death camp. All the people who got taken there were killed.'

'Most of them were killed,' says Yuli. 'Almost all of them. But it was also a work camp, and a few survived. We've been getting reports from Jewish partisan groups. Since the Nazis started losing the war, they've been marching survivors from their Polish concentration camps back to Germany.'

I struggle to take this in.

Suddenly I remember something.

The Jewish people being marched along the

lane the day I took Axel's bike. I thought they were going to a concentration camp, but they could have been coming from one.

I'm trembling so much I can hardly speak.

'I want to go there,' I say. 'To Germany. Take me there.'

Yuli hesitates again. She's starting to look like she wishes she hadn't told me.

'Felix,' she says gently. 'Why don't we make enquiries first? To save you disappointment if . . .'

'Take me there,' I say.

I'm being rude and bossy, but I'm desperate.

Yuli sighs.

'I'm sorry, Felix,' she says. 'I can't take you to Germany. There's something else I have to do. Something very important.'

'All right,' I say. 'I'll go on my own.'

'You don't have to do that,' says Yuli. 'If there was no other way for you to get there, I would go with you. But there is another way. I know some people who'll take you.'

'Partisans?' I say.

'Russian soldiers,' she says.

The town marketplace, what's left of it, is full of Russian soldiers.

And Russian tanks and lorries and ambulances and huge guns on wheels.

And hardly any Nazi soldiers. Just the few dead ones we saw in a ditch on our way in.

Yuli is standing next to one of the ambulances talking to a Russian officer. She's been doing it for ages. The rest of us are waiting at the edge of the town square with the cart.

I'm trying to see from the Russian officer's face how he feels about giving me a lift to Germany.

He's doing a lot of frowning.

Axel and Helmut are staring anxiously at the Russian soldiers too. I realise why. The Russians hate Nazis and usually kill them. Axel and Helmut have taken their Hitler Youth jackets off, even though it's freezing, but I think some of the Russians may have seen them do it.

'Hey,' I say to the others. 'Let's play football.'

They look at me as though I'm mad, but I grab the empty jewellery bag from the cart and stuff some straw into it to make a ball.

'Me and Hannah against Axel and Helmut,' I say. 'With Beryl and Faiga and Bug in goal.'

The goal is between Dom's back legs.

We start playing.

Gabriek was right, when you're feeling very stressed it is good to keep busy. Plus now that the Russian soldiers can see Axel and Helmut playing football with Jewish kids, with a bit of luck they won't want to kill them.

The score is two–two when Yuli comes over.

'Good news, Felix,' she says. 'They'll take you.'

I stare at her. The ball bounces off my head.

Hannah is very competitive and hadn't noticed I'd stopped playing.

'The Russians know where the survivors from your parents' camp were taken,' says Yuli. 'They'll make sure you get there.'

'Thank you,' I say.

I'm trembling again.

It's partly because I'm so grateful and partly because I'm having lots of other feelings.

I look at Hannah and Axel and the others. How must this be for them? Nobody can take them to find their parents because their parents are all dead. They saw the bodies with their own eyes.

Hannah looks back at me without blinking.

'Don't feel bad, Felix,' she says. 'We'd go if we were you.'

Axel and Helmut are nodding.

My eyes are filling up and I haven't even said goodbye yet.

I have to start somewhere.

I go over to Dom and hug him.

'I'm sorry,' I say to him. 'I wish I didn't have to leave you. But humans are different to horses. We need our parents. I hope you understand.'

I look into his big dark eyes and I think he does.

'I'll come back afterwards and find you,' I say. 'If I can.'

I hope this makes Dom feel better.

Yuli strokes his shoulders.

'He'll be OK,' she says. 'I'll get him a home with

174

a decent farmer. Most of the horses around here are dead, so they'll be queuing up for him.'

'Thanks,' I say.

'And once the war finishes there'll be places for kids to go,' says Yuli. 'I'll try to make sure the rest of this football team can stay together.'

'You can tell them I'm Jewish if it helps,' says Axel.

Hannah and I smile at what a silly idea that is.

Axel looks puzzled.

I leave it to Hannah to explain later.

'The partisans from the main camp are still fighting up north,' says Yuli. 'I haven't heard any news about Gabriek, but if I see him, I'll tell him where you've gone.'

'Thanks,' I say again.

I don't spoil the moment by explaining why he probably won't be that interested.

Instead I give Yuli the biggest hug I've given anybody for a long time.

She looks at me sadly.

'Good luck, Felix,' she says. 'Try not to get your hopes up too high. Most of the people on the forced marches from the concentration camps didn't survive, I have to tell you that.'

I nod, but only so she won't say anything else.

I give Hannah and Axel and Helmut and the little girls a big hug each.

'Thanks for the good protection, Felix,' says Beryl.

I try to speak but I can't. I look at Yuli and I hope she can see I'm saying the same thing to her.

I was wrong about parents.

Kids can't do without them, not even in wartime. That's why I hope Hannah and the others are as lucky as I've been and find new ones.

I've been incredibly lucky.

First Barney, then Genia, then Gabriek, and now Yuli.

Suddenly I don't want to go. I don't want to lose Yuli as well. What if I can't find Mum and Dad? What if I end up with all my parents gone? Even a lucky person like me can't expect to keep finding new ones.

Yuli sees me hesitating.

She gives me an encouraging smile.

For a moment she looks like Mum used to.

'Thank you,' I whisper to her. 'I wish you were coming with me.'

'So do I,' says Yuli quietly. 'But there's a lot of work I still have to do. After the war's over, Nazi leaders will be trying to escape. Planning new lives in other parts of the world. Pretending they never did terrible things. Some of us aren't going to let them do that.'

She kisses me on the forehead.

I'm glad she told me. It makes me feel not so bad about leaving her.

Her eyes are so soft and loving now, but one day an escaping Nazi leader will see her looking at the soft spot under his chin and suddenly he'll want his mother almost as much as I want mine.

From my pocket I take the last ring and put it in Yuli's hand.

'You might need this later,' I say. 'When you've finished all your work.'

She looks at the ring for a long time, then puts it in her pocket.

'Thank you,' she says, with just a bit of a smile.

I let her lead me over to the Russian officer.

After travelling with the Russian army for about ten minutes, I started to get anxious.

I'm in an ambulance. Not as a patient, as a passenger. Yuli must have told the Russian officer about my medical experience.

There are four Russian medical staff in here with me. And lots of medical equipment. Doctor Zajak would have cut his own leg off to have equipment like this. I bet there's enough penicillin in here to cure a horse.

As far as I can see, we're the only ambulance in this Russian army convoy.

We're passing through town after town, village after village. In every single one there are sick and injured people and animals. The streets are full of them. We should be stopping to help them.

That's what's making me anxious.

I don't want to.

I'm ashamed to admit it, but I just want us to

keep moving, to keep getting closer to Mum and Dad. If we stop to treat people, we could take weeks to get to Germany.

There'll be other ambulances coming along.

That's what I'm telling myself anyway.

'You've probably got orders,' I say hopefully to the Russian medical staff. 'To stay with the convoy and not stop unless the rest of the vehicles stop.'

I don't think these men know what I'm saying. They probably don't speak Polish. When I speak to them, they just laugh and call me *babushka*.

That's probably Russian for 'selfish young person'.

They're right, I am being selfish. But I don't care. I just want us to keep travelling.

Fast.

So far, so good. We're sticking to our daily routine.

Wake up early.

Drive all day and most of the evening.

Go to bed late.

I can't wait to be with Mum and Dad again. We've got so much to tell each other. So many sad things. But it won't be too bad, because at the same time we'll be so happy to be together.

I wonder if we'll go back to live in our old town? I hope so. I want to help Mum and Dad in our bookshop.

Books will probably be scarce for a while. Most of them get destroyed in wars, and a lot of the shelving. But Mum and Dad are really good booksellers. They'll know where to get new ones.

There's so much to think about.

For example, I'll need a new bed.

I was six the last time I lived in our flat. My old bed must be tiny. Mum and Dad believe beds have to be big enough so you can lie completely flat. It's important for sleep, and in case somebody wants to blow a raspberry on your tummy.

I peer through the ambulance window.

Look at that, there's a bed out there now. A big one sitting on a pile of rubble.

I almost ask the ambulance driver to stop, but I don't. Somebody probably owns that bed, and it wouldn't fit in here anyway.

There's another one, except it's in pieces. And it's got blood on it.

I have a worrying thought.

Will our town be like this? Houses wrecked and furniture broken and people with bombing injuries? If it is, we'll have to stock helpful books for all those things.

That's if our shop is still standing.

I don't want to think about that.

We cross the border into Germany.

I was expecting a different-looking place, but it's just like Poland. The road signs are all in German, but that's how they are in Poland too.

The Russian medical staff are tense, peering out

the ambulance windows as if they're looking for something.

Nazi soldiers probably.

I'm looking for the camp where Mum and Dad are. All I can see are more wrecked houses and villages. And miserable people sitting on rubble, looking hopeless.

Just like Poland.

It feels strange.

This is Germany, the country that invented Nazis. The country that started the war. I want to hate it, but I don't hate it as much as I thought I would.

The ambulance driver suddenly swings us off the road and into a field. The rest of the convoy carries on without us. We drive across the field and park next to a farmhouse.

What's going on?

Maybe an emergency call has come through. Maybe somebody needs an amputation or a bullet removed.

We all stand up and the Russian medical staff lift up the seats to get to the storage lockers. It must be where they keep their equipment. Scalpels and vodka and candles and saws and stuff.

I hope they can fix the problem quickly so we can get moving again. If only I spoke Russian, I could offer to help, to speed things up.

Hang on. That's not medical equipment they're taking out of the lockers.

It's guns.

'What's happening?' I say.

The medical staff don't laugh this time. They signal to me to stay in the ambulance. They say something to me loudly and crossly which I don't understand.

They go into the farmhouse with the guns.

This doesn't feel right.

I can hear screams. And that was a gunshot. What type of medical treatment involves shooting? Patients have to be held down sometimes, but not shot.

I know I should wait here. I know that would be the sensible thing. Just wait here till they've finished and then let them take me to Mum and Dad.

But they're medical professionals, and I think something's going on in that farmhouse that isn't medical or professional.

I think there are people in there who need help.

I have to go and see.

I wish I hadn't.

I wish I'd stayed in the ambulance.

At least now we've caught up with the convoy and joined onto the end of it.

I'm glad we're on our way again. I just want this trip to be over.

I never want to have anything to do with the Russian army ever again. If they're in charge of Europe now, I'm going to persuade Mum and Dad that we should go and live in America or England or Australia.

And we'll invite Yuli to come and live with us so she doesn't have to live in Russia. So she won't ever have to bump into the Russian army.

It was horrible in that farmhouse.

I'm not going to tell Mum and Dad what I saw in there. They've seen enough horrible stuff themselves, they don't need any more.

I don't even want to think about it because it makes me upset.

But I can't stop thinking about it.

And I am upset.

Which is making these men laugh.

I'm sitting here with my eyes closed, trying to ignore the men, trying not to think about the dead German women in the farmhouse, trying to think about happy things. Which isn't really working because there's been a war for the last six years, and you don't get many happy things to think about in wars.

The men are dancing around in the ambulance, hugging each other.

The ambulance is rocking from side to side, but the driver doesn't care. He's jiggling in his seat and we're weaving about all over the road.

So are all the other vehicles in the convoy.

All the Russian soldiers are firing their guns into the air and throwing their helmets around.

The war's over.

It was just on the radio. They broadcast it in about six languages, one after the other.

The Nazis have surrendered.

I know I should feel happy, but I don't.

Because I don't understand. How can these men be having a party after what they did in that farmhouse?

They're medical professionals.

Their job is to heal people, not torture people and kill them.

If that's what medical professionals do, I'm glad I'm going to be a bookseller.

After we arrived at the camp, the Russians dropped me off. They didn't stop the ambulance. Just opened the back doors and pushed me out.

Face first in the mud.

Yuli's coat protects me and Gabriek's hat does too. My legs hurt, but no more than usual.

I get up and look around. I've never seen a Nazi camp before. It's not like I expected.

The gates are wide open.

There are no Nazi guards except for three of them hanging from the gateposts. The others must have run away this morning when the war ended.

On the way here, when I thought about this moment, I imagined climbing over the fence and seeing Mum and Dad in the celebrating crowd and throwing myself into their arms.

But the camp looks almost empty. I can't see any Jewish people at all. Just Russian soldiers in bulldozers tidying up huge piles of rubbish.

I go in through the gate.

Oh.

The piles aren't rubbish, they're people.

Dead people.

Lots and lots of them.

I don't want to look.

Desperately I try to stay hopeful. I tell myself it's a big camp. Rows after rows of wooden sheds stretching away into the distance. Mum and Dad could be in any one of those sheds. And there are people inside them. Now that I'm getting closer I can hear murmuring.

I go into the first shed.

Oh.

There are hundreds of people in here. All in ragged clothes and all lying on wooden bunks. Every single person looks sick. They all need urgent medical attention.

I can't give it to them. I don't know enough. If I tried it would take me years.

I'd never find Mum and Dad.

There are a couple of Russian army doctors in the shed. At least these ones seem to be doing their best. I tell myself the people will be fine. The army doctors will fix them up. But I know that's not true. There are too many people and nowhere near enough doctors.

'Sorry,' I say as I walk along the rows of bunks, peering at the faces in the gloom. 'Sorry.'

After a while I stop saying that and say Mum

and Dad's names instead, in case anyone knows where they are.

Nobody even recognises the names.

You can't blame them. If I was sick and in pain, my eyes would probably be glazed over and I'd probably be having trouble remembering people's names too.

'Son,' screams a woman's voice.

I freeze.

A woman is staggering towards me, her arms open wide and her mouth open wide too. She's got big bones and a red face.

It's not Mum.

In the second shed, I stop saying Mum and Dad's names and start saying the name of our town instead. Yuli explained that the people in this camp are from all over Europe, so it's probably best to find people from our town first and then ask them about Mum and Dad.

These people must be from a lot of different places because nobody even recognises the name of our town.

I keep going.

Bunk after bunk after bunk.

Shed after shed after shed.

I don't know what I'll do if they're not here.

Yes I do. I'll start again. Go through all the sheds again. Just in case I missed them.

I pause for a rest. I'm almost at the end of a shed.

I've said the name of our town so many times it doesn't even sound like our town any more. I lick my lips and try to swallow so my voice won't be so croaky.

I say the name of our town again.

A hand comes out of the gloom and grabs my wrist.

I look down.

It takes me a few moments, but then relief flows through me like penicillin as I recognise the face.

Mr Rosenfeld.

Mr Rosenfeld takes a lot longer to recognise me. I don't blame him. We haven't seen each other for seven years. He looks a bit older, but I probably look totally different. I was only six when we stopped being neighbours.

'Felix Salinger,' I say again.

'Felix Salinger?' repeats Mr Rosenfeld again, still puzzled.

I nod again.

'From the bookshop,' I say.

Mr Rosenfeld's eyes widen.

'Felix Salinger,' he says.

It's not a question any more. It's something that sounds as if it amazes him.

'I'm so pleased to see you, Mr Rosenfeld,' I say.

I hardly dare say the next thing.

'Have you seen my parents?'

Mr Rosenfeld stares at me for a while.

Then his face droops.

Suddenly I feel scared and anxious. I don't want to hear what he has to say, but it's too late.

'I'm sorry, Felix Salinger,' he says. 'Your father died.'

I just stand there, holding on to the bunk.

Oh, Dad.

Slowly I start breathing again and it hurts.

You knew, I say to myself. You knew he couldn't be alive. You've known that for two years and seven months and quite a few days. Why are you torturing yourself? Why did you come here? Why didn't you go Nazi-hunting with Yuli?

'But your mother,' says Mr Rosenfeld. 'I think your mother might still be alive. She's here in this camp. Last time I saw her she was alive.'

Mr Rosenfeld insists on taking me to find Mum.

It's very kind of him because he can hardly walk. He has to hang on to bunks. And between sheds he has to hang on to me.

I'm feeling so excited I have to hang on to him too sometimes, to slow myself down.

I hate going this slow. I want to run ahead. I want to sprint through the sheds yelling Mum's name. I don't want to waste another second. We have so much to catch up on, me and Mum.

I want her arms round me now.

When you go this slow you can't help noticing that some of the people in the bunks aren't moving.

189

Or breathing.

Please, Mum. Don't be one of those poor people.

Please, Richmal Crompton, don't let her be.

I know Mum will probably be sick. I know she'll probably need medical attention. But that's all right because I've got Doctor Zajak's scalpels and other stuff with me and there's a town quite close to this camp. Towns have pawnshops, and good-quality scalpels are probably worth quite a lot these days so I'll be able to buy Mum lots of medicine.

'There,' says Mr Rosenfeld.

He's pointing with a shaky hand.

I peer at a bunk where an old lady is lying curled up breathing noisily. I look more closely because most of the bunks have several people in them, so Mum must be behind the old lady somewhere.

She's not.

I start to cry.

It's not an old lady, it's Mum.

After Mr Rosenfeld took me to Mum, he told me he'd be fine to get back to his shed on his own. Normally I would have helped him, but I didn't.

I can't leave her now.

Not after all this time.

'Thanks, Mr Rosenfeld,' I say.

Mum.

Mum, it's me, Felix.

At first I can't make the words come out. When I try to they just come out as sobs.

She's so thin. Even her skin is thin. Her hair is grey. She's not even old and her hair is grey.

'Mum,' I whisper. 'It's me.'

She looks up. It's nearly seven years since we saw each other, but she knows. She knows instantly.

'Felix,' she whispers, her eyes shining.

Her voice is quieter than a whisper. It's not even as loud as her breathing.

I kneel down and me and Mum put our arms

round each other. Because she's so thin she feels smaller than me, but only at first. Then she feels bigger than me and it's the best feeling in the world.

We stay like that in the dusty twilight of the Nazi shed for a long time.

A long, long time.

Then I tell Mum everything.

I tell her about Barney and Genia and Gabriek and Yuli. I tell her about Zelda. I tell her so much about Zelda.

Only then, when I've paused for breath because talking about Zelda always takes my breath away, do I really notice Mum's breathing.

What a struggle it is for her to do it.

How she winces every time she does.

And only then do I realise how much pain my mum is in.

'You've got to help her,' I yell at the first Russian army doctor I can find. 'She's my mother.'

I know it's rude of me and I know it's unfair. This shed is full of people in pain like Mum, some of them moaning with it, but I'm desperate and I don't care.

'She's my mum,' I shout at him again.

I can see the Russian army doctor doesn't know what I'm talking about. He doesn't understand Polish, not even when it's very loud.

He says something to me in Russian, which I don't understand. I hope it's something about speeding Mum to a special military hospital and giving her all the medicine she needs to make her better, but I doubt it.

The Russian army doctor takes me to another Russian army doctor.

'I speak Polish,' says the second doctor.

She has a strict face but kind eyes. I'm starting to think I was wrong about the Russian army. They're not all thugs.

I tell this doctor about Mum.

She listens, and comes with me to examine Mum.

Well, not examine her, just have a quick glance at her. Then she takes me outside the shed.

'I'm sorry,' she says. 'Your mother is going to die.'

I know she's wrong. I explain to her that I have extensive medical experience, and if she tells me how, I can stay with Mum and help make her better.

The doctor doesn't listen. She tells me that when people spend years in Nazi concentration camps, starvation and disease ruin their insides and when it gets as serious as it has with Mum, nothing can stop them dying.

'She would probably have died today,' says the doctor, 'if you hadn't come along.'

Exactly.

I have come along.

And I'm going to save her.

'Probably now that you're here,' says the doctor, 'she'll hang on for a few days. In agony. For your sake. If you want that.'

The doctor's eyes aren't kind any more. She's looking at me with a hard expression and biting her lip.

I want her to be wrong about Mum being in agony, but she's not.

'Mum wouldn't be in pain if you gave her something to take it away,' I say.

'If we had anything, we would,' says the doctor.

I show her Doctor Zajak's scalpels.

She agrees they're good scalpels, but when I ask her how much she thinks I'd get for them in the local town, or how much medicine I could swap them for, she says I wouldn't get anything because the people in town are starving and they want food not scalpels.

I put the scalpels away.

The doctor looks at me for a moment more, her face very sad now, then she goes.

I stand there and think about everything she said.

I stand in the cold evening wind for a long time.

A long, long time.

After I finished thinking about what the Russian army doctor said, I went back to Mum and lay down with her on the bunk and put my arms round her. As soon as I did, I knew the doctor was wrong.

Mum has nodded off.

Her breathing is gentler and her face has started to relax.

She's starting to get better already.

Then she wakes up with a jolt as if she's just remembered something and her breathing gets loud and painful again and she turns and stares at me anxiously.

'It's all right, Mum,' I say. 'I'm here.'

Mum coughs.

Not just a little cough, a big one that makes her whole body go stiff and I can see she's crying with the pain.

'I won't leave you,' she whispers when the cough

finally stops. 'I won't leave you again.'

I hold her as tight as I can without hurting her more.

'Dad didn't want to leave you,' she says. 'When he died, the last thing he said was your name.'

We lie there, Mum struggling to breathe, me struggling to keep my tears as quiet as I can. I'm crying partly for poor Dad, and partly for poor Mum, and partly because I know I'm wrong.

The doctor is right.

And now I know what I have to do.

I think about the first time Mum and Dad left me. How hard it must have been for them to take me to that Catholic orphanage and leave me there. How much they must have wanted to hang on to me.

But they didn't.

They let me go.

For my sake.

I kiss Mum gently on the cheek and tell her a story.

It's a story about Gabriek. How well he's looked after me. How he's going to look after me again now the war's over.

I tell her how good he is at mending things. I tell her about lots of the things he's mended. I tell her how we're going to meet up soon and mend things together.

It's mostly a true story, but like all stories it has some imagination in it.

Some make-believe.

I don't tell her that me and Gabriek won't ever see each other again.

By the time I've finished, Mum is asleep.

After I finally went to sleep, still with my arms round Mum, I had a dream.

Mum waking up.

Me already awake.

'Bye, Mum,' I whisper to her. 'I'll always love you. Thanks for waiting, but you don't have to any more.'

'Goodbye, dear Felix,' she whispers back, her voice so quiet, so frail, so loving. 'Thank you for coming into our lives.'

Dreams are like stories. We have them for the same reason we have stories.

To help us know things and feel better about them.

After I woke up, and saw my dream had come true, I stayed with Mum's body for a long time.

So still, so peaceful.

No more painful breathing.

No more coughing agony.

Just my tears.

My friend Zelda once said that tears are how we give love a wash, so it doesn't go mouldy.

Bye, dear Mum.

If you see Zelda, tell her she's right.

I tell the Russian army doctor, the one who speaks Polish, what's happened.

She squeezes my shoulder and gives me a kind look. She explains that this camp has two funerals a day, and she can fit Mum into the morning one.

'Thanks,' I say.

I don't feel quite so thankful when I see that the grave is a big pit that has been dug by a bulldozer, and that the bulldozer is also what they use to put the bodies into the grave.

'No,' I say.

I go and pick up Mum's body and carry it down into the grave and lay it gently in one corner away from the tangled bodies.

I kiss her one last time.

'Thank you for being my mum,' I whisper. 'And for giving me my life.'

Then I scoop up handfuls of earth and gently cover her with it so when the bulldozer fills in the grave, she won't have great lumps of dirt dropping directly onto her.

I stand at the edge of the grave watching the bulldozer doing its work.

All those people, all those families, all gone.

I close my eyes. I try to have happy memories of me and Mum and Dad, but I'm not ready for that.

I do some more crying instead.

I don't know why everyone gets so ecstatic when a war ends. People keep dying anyway. When I think about that, what I really feel like doing is finding a hole somewhere and hiding away from all the sad things in the world.

A hand touches me gently on the shoulder.

It must be Mr Rosenfeld. That is so kind. I saw him at Mum's funeral, even though walking over here would have been very difficult for him.

I turn to thank him.

But it's not Mr Rosenfeld.

It's the Russian army doctor who speaks Polish. She's holding something out to me.

My compass.

'This was on your mother's bunk,' she says with a sympathetic smile.

'Thank you,' I say.

As she goes, I stare at the compass in my hand. I think about Gabriek. I think about the other people I've met who are like him.

Kind people.

Mending people.

Suddenly I don't want to hide away after all.

After I explained to the kind Russian army doctor what I wanted to do, she checked with her superior officer and after a bit of discussion and quite a lot of frowning he nodded and I started work.

As a medical assistant.

Well, more of a nurse really.

The Russian army doctors don't really like being assisted, so I work mostly on my own. Trying to help some of the people in the sheds feel a bit better.

Helping them have a wash if they want one.

Helping them eat some food if there is any.

Talking to them if they feel like it.

Holding their hand.

'Felix.'

I wake up.

My head is resting against the upright plank at the end of a bunk.

I feel terrible. The man whose hand I'm holding

today is Mr Rosenfeld. He wants to talk but I must have nodded off.

I apologise and explain that I'm not getting much sleep because my bed is in the hut where they keep the spare parts for the bulldozers and it's very noisy because the bulldozer mechanics often have to work at night.

Mr Rosenfeld manages to smile. After a while, when he stops wheezing and can speak, he says he understands.

He's nice.

He reminds me a bit of Dad. Even when Mr Rosenfeld's having pain, his eyes are gentle like Dad's were. But I never saw Dad this thin or with such sore skin or trembling hands.

We talk for a while, and after that I go and get Mr Rosenfeld some more water, but when I come back he's unconscious.

I fetch a Russian army doctor who looks at Mr Rosenfeld and shakes his head. I sit with Mr Rosenfeld for a long time, holding his hand as it slowly goes cold.

Then I go outside to cry.

The kind army doctor who speaks Polish has explained to me that crying is important when you work with people who die. If you cry each time, it helps you keep going.

Each time I go to the same place.

The corner of the big grave where Mum is buried.

I've made a little headstone for her and Dad out of wood, in the shape of a book.

That's where I do my crying.

I hope the people who die don't mind me sharing my tears.

'Beautiful compass,' whispers Misha.

He should know, he's a sailor, which is pretty unusual. There aren't many Jewish sailors. I've worked in this camp for nearly two weeks and Misha is the first one I've met.

I'm glad I've got the compass to show him because when I told him my name he got upset. He tried to get out of his bunk, but he's not strong enough.

I didn't understand at first why he was so upset. Then Misha told me his father was called Felix too and was a sailor as well before the Nazis burned him to death in a synagogue.

Misha is nineteen, but his hair is completely grey.

Sometimes he sees things.

'Daddy,' he yells, grabbing my arms and staring at me, his eyes so big I can see where his eye sockets bleed a bit sometimes.

We've only been talking for about an hour, but this is the third time he's done that.

'Misha,' I say gently. 'I'm not your father, I'm your friend.'

Misha starts crying.

Then his sobs turn into shudders, big ones, and they don't stop and I look around for a doctor but before I can find one it's too late.

I close Misha's eyes and fold one of his hands around the compass and I try to get up and go outside but I can't so I just sit here.

I don't know how much longer I can do this. I want to be a kind person and a mending person, but I don't know how much longer I can do this on my own.

A hand touches me on the shoulder.

I know who it is. One of the Russian army doctors, reminding me that if I'm going to cry, I should do it outside so I don't upset the other people in here.

I turn round to show the doctor I'm a medical professional and I'm perfectly capable of controlling myself. But when I see who it is, I don't control myself at all.

It isn't an army doctor, it's Gabriek.

After helping me at the camp for a few days, Gabriek persuaded me I'd done as much there as one person could, and explained we had other important work to do, and so we made one last visit to Mum and Dad's memorial and then we left.

First we came here, to the old partisan camp.

As we approached through the forest, I thought I could smell smoke. But it must have been a sad memory playing tricks, because the camp is deserted.

We look inside the hollow tree.

Yes.

Everything's untouched.

Gabriek's violin. Genia's photo frame. My books and important drawings and the locket Zelda gave me.

'That's lucky,' I say.

Gabriek looks almost as happy as he did when he found me.

'Very lucky,' he says.

'Very lucky indeed,' says an unfriendly voice.

I hear a sound I recognise. I can see Gabriek recognises it too. The safety catch on a gun.

Tall skinny scowling Szulk steps out from behind a tree.

'God help us,' he says. 'Those stupid Nazis couldn't do anything right, could they? Couldn't even get rid of all you Jews.'

He raises his gun and points it at Gabriek's head.

'He's not Jewish,' I say frantically. 'It's just me.'

'Jew-lovers are just as bad,' says Szulk. 'Poland doesn't need any of you.'

I see his finger start to tighten on the trigger.

Gabriek gives a grunt, and hurls himself at the gun. Szulk steps back and smashes Gabriek to the ground with his rifle butt.

While Szulk is doing that, I reach into my shirt and get my fingers inside the rolled-up cotton vest and pull out a scalpel and lunge at him.

Szulk sees me coming and sways to one side so I slash wildly and Szulk screams. He drops to his knees. He fumbles with the buttons of his shirt and gets it half off. Across the front of his chest is a vivid red line.

He swears at me and tries to stand up, using his rifle as a prop, but it slips out of his fingers and he falls onto his back.

Now's my chance.

The soft part under his chin is waiting for me.

I grip the scalpel and stand over him.

Szulk's eyes are bulging and his lips are blue. He's going into shock. Doctor Zajak and me used to see this all the time.

One quick incision and he'll never be a threat to anybody again.

Szulk's eyes are pleading with me. I try not to look at them. But I can't forget what Yuli said, about him losing his family.

Gabriek groans. He's sitting up, rubbing his back and watching me.

'Your choice,' he says.

He's right, it is my choice.

I love Gabriek for letting me have it. It's why I'm so lucky to have him as a friend.

I pull the candle out of my shirt, borrow Gabriek's matches and his bottle of vodka, and do a clean and heat on Szulk's cut chest. Soon the bleeding has almost stopped.

Gabriek holds Szulk down and smothers his howls while I sew up his wound with some thread from his pants.

Then we break his gun and walk away.

'Hey,' yells Szulk. 'You can't leave me.'

'Felix is a medical man, not a travel agent,' says Gabriek. 'The police'll provide transport.'

We head along the forest path towards town. After a bit, I make Gabriek stop while I check his back for damage.

Bruising and skin abrasions, but otherwise fine.

'You're going to be a good surgeon one day,' says Gabriek as we walk on.

I look at him.

He means it. It's not just a story he's making up.

I hope he's right.

'Education,' says Gabriek. 'Get as much as you can. You'll need years of it before people will let you cut them open without complaining.'

Gabriek's right about that, and because he's my friend, I think he'll do everything he can to help me get it.

But first, we have work to do. Things need mending. Too much of the world has been broken. We have to get busy, me and Gabriek, doing our bit to help fix things up.

Plenty of time for everything else after.

Dear Reader

After *is the fourth book about Felix.*

In Once *and* Then, *Felix is a ten-year-old Jewish boy struggling to survive in Nazi-occupied Poland in 1942. He and his dearest friend, six-year-old Zelda, are caught up in that terrible time we call the Holocaust.*

In the third book, Now, *Felix is an elderly man in the present day. Through the eyes of his granddaughter, also called Zelda, we see Felix confront some of the pain of his childhood while he and the new Zelda face a new struggle to survive – in Australia's biggest bushfire.*

When I finished Now, *I thought my work with Felix and the two Zeldas was complete. But Felix didn't agree. And so* After *is set in 1945, the final year of World War Two. Felix was right. These months turn out to be a momentous time in his young life.*

For their help with After, *my heartfelt thanks to Laura Harris, Sarah Hughes, Heather Curdie, Tony Palmer, Anna Fienberg and Belinda Chayko.*

If you haven't read Once, Then *or* Now, *please don't worry. I've tried to write these stories so they can be read in any order. If you read* After *first, you'll know some of what happens in* Once *and* Then, *but not too much.*

Like the other three Felix stories, *After* came from my imagination, but it was inspired by a period of history that was all too real.

I couldn't have written any of these stories without first reading many books about the Holocaust. Books full of the real voices of the people who lived and struggled and loved and died, or, as just a few of them did, survived in that terrible time.

I also read about the generosity and bravery of the people who risked their lives to resist the Nazis, and to shelter others, often children.

You can find details of some of my research reading on my website. I hope you get to share some of it and help keep alive the memory of these people.

This story is my imagination trying to grasp the unimaginable.

Their stories are the real stories.

Morris Gleitzman
August 2012

www.morrisgleitzman.com

Then

I had a plan for me and Zelda.

Pretend to be someone else.

Find new parents.

Be safe forever.

Then the Nazis came.

**The brilliant, moving sequel to *Once*.
Then has also received many literary honours and
children's choice awards.**

'. . . an exquisitely told, unflinching and courageous novel.'
The Age

'Gleitzman's Felix and Zelda are two of the finest and
sure-to-endure characters created in recent times.'
Hobart Mercury

'[Gleitzman] has accomplished something extraordinary,
presenting the best and the worst of humanity without stripping
his characters of dignity or his readers of hope.'
Guardian

Now

Once I didn't know about my grandfather Felix's scary childhood.

Then I found out what the Nazis did to his best friend Zelda.

Now I understand why Felix does the things he does.

At least he's got me.

My name is Zelda too.

This is our story.

Now continues to receive many literary honours and children's choice awards in Australia and overseas.

'*Now* is an edifying and tender, nuanced novel from
an exceptionally compassionate author.'
The Age

'Gleitzman has a special way of seeing the world through the eyes
of a child, and generations of readers are grateful to him for it.'
West Australian

'It is beautifully written, stunning in its simplicity
and powerful in its sensitivity. Read it and it is sure
to haunt you for ever.'
Scotsman

Laugh, cry and escape
with
Morris GLEITZMAN

Two stories of friendship, adventure, courage and ball control

'Moving and page-turning'
– Sunday Times

'A brilliantly funny writer'
– Sunday Telegraph

morrisgleitzman.com

puffin.co.uk

It all started with a Scarecrow.

Puffin is seventy years old.
Sounds ancient, doesn't it? But Puffin has never been
so lively. We're always on the lookout for the next big
idea, which is how it began all those years ago.

Penguin Books was a big idea from the mind of
a man called Allen Lane, who in 1935 invented
the quality paperback and changed the world.
**And from great Penguins, great Puffins grew,
changing the face of children's books forever.**

The first four Puffin Picture Books were hatched in 1940 and the
first Puffin story book featured a man with broomstick arms called
Worzel Gummidge. In 1967 Kaye Webb, Puffin Editor, started the
Puffin Club, promising to **'make children into readers'.**
She kept that promise and over 200,000 children became
devoted Puffineers through their quarterly instalments of
Puffin Post, which is now back for a new generation.

Many years from now, we hope you'll look back and
remember Puffin with a smile. **No matter what your age
or what you're into, there's a Puffin for everyone.**
The possibilities are endless, but one thing is for sure:
whether it's a picture book or a paperback, a sticker book
or a hardback, **if it's got that little Puffin
on it – it's bound to be good.**